I0749198

I Believe In Butterflies

Also by Marian L. Thomas

The Naya Monà Series
Color Me Jazzmyne
My Father's Colors
Strings of Color

Stand-Alone Titles
Aqua Blue
Blue Butterfly

Children's Books
Things Sasha Learned From Her Dog Winston

I Believe In *Butterflies*

Marian L. Thomas

Atlanta

L.B. Publishing
400 West Peachtree St NW
#4-858
Atlanta, GA 30308

www.lbpublishingbooks.com

Printed in the United States of America.

First Edition: May 2017

For Speaking events, go to www.marianlthomas.com

Library of Congress Control Number: 2016962436

Thomas, Marian L.
I Believe In Butterflies / Marian L. Thomas —1st. ed.
ISBN 978-0-984-89679-0 (paperback edition) 1. Family secrets —Fiction. 2. Friendship—Fiction. 3. Women's—Fiction. 4. Domestic—Fiction.

To Winston—The Best Dog Ever.
14.5 Years was not enough.

Acknowledgments

Many thanks to my wonderful husband of seventeen years—thank you for always keeping me focused on the most important things. To my sister, thank you for always reminding me that I can accomplish anything. To my dear friends who are always at the finish line, cheering me on—thank you. To my spiritual family members—thank you for always keeping me grounded. To my mother-in-law, stepfather, aunts, uncles, cousins, nephews, and nieces—I love each of you. To every person involved in the production of this book—thank you. To all my co-workers who encouraged and supported me—thank you. To every bookstore who sells my works—thank you! To the bloggers who feature me or my books—thank you so much! To the radio stations, newspapers and online websites that help promote my work—thank you.

To EDC-Creations, Ella Curry, and the Black Diamond PR Firm —thank you.

To every reader—thank you for your kind words, for your book reviews, for spreading the word about my books, for posting and for sharing my works via social media. To every book club—thank you for selecting one of my books as your monthly selection. I am grateful for each of you.

To my mother who has loved and supported me—thank you.

Marian L. Thomas

Website: www.marianlthomas.com

Facebook: www.facebook.com/marian.l.thomas

Twitter: www.twitter.com/marianlthomas01

Instagram: www.instagram.com/marianlthomas09

PROLOGUE

I'm about to take my last breath.

I suppose not everybody gets to write down their last thoughts before they die. But since you know I always got to get the last word; I'm writing this down for you baby girl. I reckon that's something. In the end, I figure we all still trying to find something to leave behind, something that reminds folks that we once walked the good ground and took a deep breath for seventy or eighty years. I ain't gonna lie; my last thoughts are probably something one wishes they could keep locked up inside them. Shoot, you probably wondering why I'm telling it. Heck, I reckon right about now, you're wondering why I don't just take it with me. I don't know really. I guess I just felt like my bones are tired of trying to find the right, forgiving water to stop the hurt.

As my daddy used to say, "Truth, let the heart speak it."

I know I quote from him a lot. But that's what good hand-me-down wisdom does for you. I hope I handed some down to you that you can use.

I pray I'm going to give you something to keep in that beautiful heart of yours.

Anywho, I was supposed to be telling you something, so I reckon I better get on with it.

My truth.

I didn't believe you at first. I didn't believe the truth that dripped from the lips of my child. But I need you to know baby girl…I need you to know that in the end, I believed everything and I was sorry.

ONE
Emma Lee Baker

Some people say that I'm crazy. A crazy ole black woman with nothing better to do than stand on the bridge during the heat of the day and stare at the fish that swim by in the crisp blue water.

I ain't crazy. I just like staring at freedom.

I like looking at the fish swimming from one end of the river, clear up to the other. Ain't nobody worried about what color they are or if they be big fish or small fish. Ain't nobody worried about any of those things when it comes to the fish.

Folks been fishing in that water for years and my fish ain't never lost their freedom.

I reckon that if God gave them fish their freedom, then that's how it was meant to be for all people.

He didn't make them better than he made us.

Anywho, as for little ole me, it seems folks around here tend to take notice of my coming and going. I reckon it's my fault. I mean, if I hadn't been standing on that bridge that day, I might not have seen it. The dead body that is.

It was a female. A young girl. I reckon that she was no more than fourteen or so. Her blond hair was wrapped around her neck like it was the thing that choked the poor life out of her.

At first, I stared at her for a good while. It might have been a few hours. I guess I just got carried away. Wondering how long she'd been in the water with my fish. It wasn't until Ms. Mary came up to see if I was finally going to jump in and end my crazy ole life, that I realized I ought to say something.

Ms. Mary started screaming when she saw it. Typical for white women. Always dramatic. Black folks around here been seeing dead bodies for centuries.

Anywho, next thing I knew, the Sheriff and the rest of our small police department come raging down the dirt road, blocking all the traffic that by then, had done multiplied on the Thompson Mill Bridge.

Word carries fast around here—Barrow County, Georgia. It doesn't matter which side of the Seaboard Air Line Railroad you rest ya head on.

Jimmy, our Sheriff—started asking me questions, once his dirty little boots hit the pavement. Questions that I didn't have the answers to. I told him that I didn't know anything. That I just saw the body, I didn't put it there.

He told me to go home and to not leave town.

Jimmy is not different from his daddy; they're both short, stocky, and almost bald. I think that's the reason Jimmy always walking around town with a hat on. Jimmy loves himself some spotlight. Always trying to get himself in the papers with a big grin on his face and his hands on his gun. I believe he loves to turn them sirens on just so he has a reason to drive like he ain't got no sense.

He ain't got none, truth be told, but still, he talks to me like I ain't got none either. I always liked Jimmy, he got a kind heart and I been knowing him since he was a baby. However, there are plenty of times I want to tell him that just because I am twice his age—seventy-six, that doesn't mean I can't put thoughts together. I ain't never said this to his face, 'cause even at seventy-six, I know that they could still take my old butt to jail and then, my daughter who lives in Chicago would have to come and bail my butt out. I reckon it would take her about three days or so to do it, but eventually, her conscience would kick her in the rear, and she'd pick up that fancy car she drives and come see about her mama.

Yes, three days ought to do it.

She and I don't speak much. She thinks her bridges done got to high and mighty to come back to her roots. The truth is—on the day she crossed over from the black side of the railroad tracks and walked a couple of miles to board the only train we got, I never wanted her to come back. Just call. We get along so much better on the phone for the one or two minutes we manage to have a conversation.

Honour is a smart girl, so I could never understand why she went off and got a fancy college degree only to open some high and mighty hair salon all the way up in Chicago. They don't even have sweet tea in Chicago. I make a mean pitcher of sweet tea. Everyone in town will swear to it.

My child would too. She just done forgot what her mama's tea feels like running down her throat, that's all. It's like, as soon as she finished high school, she had her bags and the real sense her daddy, and I tried to instill in her, rearing to go.

Her salon was in the papers a lot 'cause some of them celebrities you see on the television like to sit in her chair.

The local paper here wrote a story about her. It made the front page. It seems it was headline news that a black girl from Barrow County made something of herself in the big city of Chicago. I still have that article. In fact, I have every article about her that has even been written.

I named her Honour and Jean, my husband, gave her the middle name—Blue because it's his favorite color. We fought about it for most of the time I was pregnant with her, but, once that child was born, I didn't see any point.

It was a rough pregnancy. One that nearly ended me since the doctors say I got small hips, but she came into the world as Honour Blue Baker, forty-one years ago. I remember when the doc slapped her on the butt to get her to cry, she gave him an 'how dare ya kind of look.'

Only my child would never say 'ya' in her life.

She still just as strong-minded today as she was then. It was inherited, she got it honestly from my Jean.

I came from a long line of cooks, maids, babysitters, shoe shiners, and a generation that believed in birthing babies like they were going to get money for doing so. I could never understand why they kept pumping out their children when they knew good and well that they were poor. But I reckon that if my mother had of stopped, I wouldn't be here today. I was her last.

She gave her last breath just to so I could take my own.

As for me, I only had one child. Honour came just when I thought my ovaries had gone dry. I was plum shocked, to be honest with ya. I had come to reckon that I just didn't get the blessing all the other women in my family got. In fact, Jean and I had gotten mighty use to it being just he and I, after years of trying. But low and behold, at thirty-five, I delivered a healthy baby girl with a lush of wavy black hair. I remember Jean hollering and carrying on like he done won some money or something. He bonded with her the moment she reached out and grabbed his finger. Not too many daddies like that nowadays. Shame, though, since little girls need a father they can hold hands with.

TWO

Like having Honour, I got married late in my life. Jean and I were married in 1956. I was 30 years-old. Folks around town thought I was gonna be single forever. Shoot, truth be told, so did I. My sisters all got married; it seemed not long after their cycles started. My two brothers snatched them up a wife when they each turned eighteen and started their own baby-making houses. I met Jean one day as I went to the candy store to buy myself some peppermint. He had just moved from the county over with his Uncle. He was a tall, slender man with black wavy hair. I knew he had some white in him 'cause most black folks around here didn't have wavy hair like that. Plus, his skin was light. I mean like that bright-light kind. My daddy called him, "high-yellow." I called him handsome. He came stepping into the candy store like he owned the place. He had on shiny black leather shoes and a crisp white shirt that was tucked neatly into his perfectly creased pants. I wondered if he was coming from some religious service or a funeral dressed like that in the mid-part of the day. He saw me standing at the counter with an A-line black and white polka-dot dress on. My hair was pulled back and tucked neatly in a bun. For some reason that day, I had done stuck a red flower in it. The sun was shining brightly, and I guess I had just needed to show my appreciation.

Jean didn't say anything to me at first. He waited until I had done paid and then he followed me out the store.

Typical of a man is what I had thought at first.

Anywho, we both stood there, staring at the dirt road as if it was gonna talk for us until he did something that I had never heard a man do before, he started singing to me. I mean, lungs open wide and everything. People stopped to listen. Even the white folks. His voice was like a pleasant aroma that one smelled from the roses when they are in full bloom.

My daddy used to say that one should never walk by a bed of roses and not stop to tell them how thankful you were for them sharing their natural given ability with you.

Jean Baker's voice was the kind that slid down my bones. It oozed out through my toes and made me want to run down the street butt-naked screaming.

I gave my heart to him at that moment, and I was mighty happy when he didn't return it.

We were married six months later.

The fact that he sang for his living didn't bother me. I reckon that God gave him that voice and he was only using it to make a living, not rob nobody. My Daddy, however, at the time, didn't think it was right for a man to make a living that way. He wanted Jean to get a job in the cotton mill, but Jean had resolved in his heart that he was never stepping foot in a cotton mill. His father had done worked most of his younger days in one, only to take home two to three dollars a day. Jean's daddy spent the rest of his life in prison after he came home and found his wife with another man. Her name was Jeannie Baker. She was hooked on the bottle and men, and loved both of them more than she loved her own husband or son for that matter. Word has it that Jean got his voice from her. People say that when she opened her mouth, she sounded like butter.

I've seen a picture of her. She was even lighter than my Jean with long curly hair, a rather thin frame, and thin lips.

Jean swore she was black.

You would think that with all that sadness caught up in your soul, one's heart would be cold. But not my Jean. Don't get me wrong, he had his moments. There were nights when he'd sit in the darkness and just stare out like he was back there again. Rolling around in the past.

It would break my heart, but I learned to let him roll around as long as he needed. My daddy used to say that "the past, is the past, and remembering it, ain't always bad when you use it to make something out of yourself."

My Jean did.

My daddy came to respect him for it.

Jean was a wonderful, hard-working man who bought me the house that I still live in. It is fully paid for. Something else unheard of around here.

He died exactly ten years ago, June 5, 1992, on the same day that Honour opened the doors to her hair salon. It was the first, and only time, he and I ever traveled outside of Barrow County. He had to see his baby girl. He suffered a heart attack that evening as we were waiting for Honour to pick us up from the hotel we were staying in.

Honour was thirty-one at the time.

Lord, I swear the two of them were like popcorn and butter. She and I, however, are more like burnt toast and year old jam. I've tried to get along with that child, but, she's too strong-willed for my blood.

But I love her. She knows this. Give my life for my child. Strong-willed or not, she will always be that little girl who played in the dirt with the blue dress on that I slaved for hours to make.

I reckon I should have called and told her what had happened on the bridge that day. I guess I was still fighting to get the image of that young child out of my mind.

Ms. Mary was the one to bring me home. She figured I was too distraught to walk. She is the one crazy if you ask me, but since ain't nobody asking, I ain't never said it out loud to no one. I have learned in my seventy-six years of living here in Barrow County to keep my opinions about people to myself.

I guess it was around seven when Ms. Mary called to tell me that the police had found a piece of paper with the King's address on it, wrapped up in the hand of that young dead girl and how the police thought she was somehow related to them.

My old eyes had done rested on her sweet and innocent face as it stared up at me from the water, and I didn't see any resemblance.

But, my eyes ain't always right.

Mildred and Paul King passed away two years back. They died within months of each other from cancer. Their house and all their money went to the State since there was no registered next of kin. It was a sad thing to consider, but true. I hope Honour come and claim me as her mama when I go. I ain't got no money, but I hope she takes the house and keeps it for her own children, although Ms. High and Mighty swear she ain't gonna give me no grandbabies and at forty-one-years-old, I started to believe she wasn't lying to me. Plus, she says she's too busy to date and marriage ain't in her plan.

That girl doesn't know that love ain't ever in the plan. Love is what happens to you. It's like a thief that comes in your life and takes your heart off to that place of sweet dreams, a touch of hard times and blissfulness every time you look into the eyes of the one you've done given your heart to.

Anywho, I stayed away from feeding my fish for a few days, but then my bones started missing them, so I decided to get back to my daily routine. Besides, I'm a firm believer that freedom must be fed.

THREE

The sun was tapping me on the shoulders as I wandered down the dirt road that was gonna lead me to the bridge. Stores in town were opening in a few hours. I cut through the back of the town so I could get myself a small glimpse of good ole Mr. Blackman, the town butcher. I might be old, but I still got decent eyesight, and he is a mighty fine man. Good natured as well. He's always at his store before the birds open their eyes. His wife passed away some years back. I reckon it hard on him to have a name like 'Blackman' when he is white as the snow that falls on our roofs and roads in the winter.

I ain't never in my life dated a white man, but ole Mr. Blackman could have a woman like me thinking differently. Old age makes you lonely, and I guess that loneliness will have you reaching out for anything, black, white, pink or purple. I figure, as long as they can provide good conversation, make your heart laugh and help fill your final days with a smile; it doesn't matter what color their skin is, although I admit I ain't always felt that way.

I have been living in Georgia all my life. Seen black folks hung. Seen black folks looked down upon. But, I've also seen white folks that have treated black folks with kindness. The Kings were like that. They were from the North by way of New York. Came to Georgia when I was in my twenties. I reckon they were about forty or so. Back then, white folks here didn't like them because they treated me and others like me, the way God meant them too. Like humans.

Mildred King was a short woman with long blond hair. She had a pointed nose and a slight face. She spoke with ease and mildness. Never once can I remember her raising her voice at anyone. Mr. King was tall. I reckon he was about three inches or so taller than Mildred. He owned the candy store that I loved to go into. It was the only one back then that sold peppermint.

They were rich or should I say...richer than any family that had lived in Barrow County during that time. Some say that Mr. King used to be an attorney in New York, but I always took that to be nothing more than gossip. However, he was smart. So, I reckon the gossip could've had some truth to it.

My daddy used to always tell me that rich folks had beds filled with secrets. I use to take that sought of talk literally. I often spent way too much time wondering how you sleep on secrets.

I reckon it was about seven in the morning when I finally come to the bridge. My fish come swimming up to me as soon as I had done pulled their food out of my pocket and began throwing it in the water. I asked them about the white girl and what they knew about her, but they felt the same way I did with all the questions- they only saw her floating in their water, they didn't put her there. I swear they told me that. Well, at least in my mind, I'd swear I had heard my fish say it.

Anywho, I was standing on the bridge and looking down into the water, loving how crystal clear it is when something caught the corner of my eye. The light coming off it was so bright that I struggled to make out what it was. So, I start walking toward the edge of the bridge, down by the rocks to see if I can get a better look.

The sun had me squinting like a fool to keep whatever it was in my sight. As I began to get closer, I could hear the water like I've never heard it before. The current was running fast down the stream. My fish moved downstream with me. I grabbed hold of the edge of a column of the bridge and tried to lean my body so I could reach out my hand and grab whatever it is that continued to blind me with its light. My feet had done lost their balance once or twice, and I just knew I was gonna end up like that white girl—floating down the river of freedom with my arms stretched out toward my fish.

I tried repositioning my body so I could see it better. A bird was hovering above. I wanted to tell that bird that I wasn't gonna be his meal. In fact, if he had of kept messing with me, he would have been mine. My daddy had taught me how to pluck them feathers when I was just a child. Those types of skills come back to you when they need too. If he had of kept messing with me, he would have found out.

It seems like the moment I had done reached out for it again, the water started coming faster. I could see my fish looking at me, wondering what in the world my crazy ole behind was trying to do out there on those rocks.

The bird was still there too, but he kept his distance.

Sun was still hot, bright, and glaring in my eyes.

Thirty minutes later, after my arm had just about fallen off, I finally held it in my hands.

It was an old gold locket.

I slipped it inside my dress as old women do, and that's when it happened.

FOUR

White walls.

White, dingy, dry-looking walls and ceiling tiles that looked like they were older than me. That's what I saw as I opened my eyes. There was also a nurse. Although I could barely make out her face, I could hear her breathing.

Snoring, actually.

"Child?" I whispered.

I got nothing

"Child!"

She jumped when she finally heard my voice.

When she lifted her head up, I recognized her. Rosa was new to town and to nursing. Two months now at the hospital. She had big lips, slim hips, and hair down to her butt that she dyes red every three weeks or so 'cause she thinks that goes with her brown skin tone. Nobody got the nerve to tell her the truth about her hair. She also has three kids at home, and a husband that has done ran off with her neighbor about six months ago. That's why they say she moved to Barrow County.

I can't blame her for this. We all running from something. For some, it is people. For others, it is themselves.

Some say she's bitter. Some say she's kind. I still hadn't decided, but I will say that everybody ain't fit to be a nurse, but here in Barrow County, nursing provides a decent living.

Rosa lives not too far from me. She is renting ole man Sutherlands' home for way too much, but you ain't heard that from me. The Sutherlands' have always been no good and money hungry.

"Mrs. Baker, you're awake?" She finally says.

I had to strain to see her. My eyelids felt like a pound or two had been sitting on top of them.

"I reckon so since I'm talking to ya."

"I'll go get the doctor."

"How long I been in here?"

"Ma'am?"

I always hated repeating myself. "How long I've been in here?"

"Five days, ma'am. You've been in a coma for five days and today is Tuesday."

It took a moment or two for them words to sink in, but then I remembered something…I reached up and realized I didn't have my wig on.

"Child, you let me lay in this here bed for five days without my wig?"

"It's right here. Your daughter took it off this morning to braid your hair."

"Honour is here?" I placed my wig on.

"Yes, ma'am. I believe Ms. Baker just went to shower and change, but I'm sure she'll be back in a few minutes."

I started feeling my chest.

"Ma'am, you okay?"

"No child, I ain't. I have been robbed."

"Ma'am?"

"You heard me. I said, I have been robbed."

"Maybe I can help you find what you think was stolen."

"Think? No child, I know." I reach down into my bra, but I didn't feel anything. "My locket is gone. I want my locket. I hit my doggone head for it and fought a bird for it, so I reckon that it belongs to me, so you go find where they done put my locket."

"Let me go get the doctor."

"I didn't ask you to go get the doctor, child, I told you to go find where they done put my locket!"

"Calm down, Mrs. Baker."

"Child, I will be calm when I get what belongs to me back. Now you go take your young self out of this room and gets my locket back."

My daughter walked into the room, and I stopped my fussing with Rosa over my lost locket, but I gave her a look that tells her that I'm not done. I still want my locket. Rosa turned her nose up at me and walked out the room, but I don't care. All I know is that she had better not walk her young broke tail back in this here room without my locket.

"You seen my locket?"

My daughter sits down by my bed and reaches down and picks up her purse. She then pulls out the locket, and I sighed in relief. I ain't gonna apologize to Rosa, but I'm glad to see I hadn't banged my head for nothing.

"I haven't seen you in years, and the first thing you do is ask me about some locket Mama?"

I ignore her and reach for my locket.

"Hello, Mama." My daughter says as she pulls the locket back toward her. I stare at her for a second. My eyes resting on her face. She looks so much like her father. Thick wavy hair hanging down her back. I ain't got much left on mine and all of it done turned gray. Honour got dark hazel eyes that I'm trying to see behind. She got his height too. She's been hovering around five seven since she was in elementary.

I give her the 'you had better give me my locket if you know what's best,' look. She places it on the nightstand and stares at me.

"You scared me, Mama."

"Why?"

"You were in a coma, Mama. The doctors didn't know if you were going to wake up and then the police kept coming by and asking questions about some girl they say you found in the river."

I smiled. I was glad my daughter was worried, at least I know she cares about her mama.

"I don't know why they keep asking me questions about that girl. I told them I only found her there, I didn't put her there."

"Is this her locket?" She held the locket up.

"I found it by the rocks, so I suppose so." I try reaching for it again, but she pulls it away. I feel like snatching my wig off and reminding her behind that I'm the mama, but I decide to go along with her foolishness for a bit more.

"Then you should give it to the police, it might be evidence that can help them."

"It's mine, I found it."

"Mama, it's evidence. You have to turn it in."

"I don't have to do nothing but eat, sleep and feed my fish." I finally snatch my locket out of her hands. She gives me a mean look, but I don't care. I'm the mama. "So, you try to open it." I ask, in my 'I won' mother's voice.

She lets out a long sigh. "I'm more worried about you, than trying to open some locket. You took a nasty hit, Mama."

"Girl, it's probably just a scratch, them doctors always making a mountain out of a pebble so they can get more money out of ya."

"You were in a coma, Mama, they had a right to make a mountain."

"Yeah, you've told me that already. When the doctor say I can get up and out of this here place? I ain't got money like you, Honour, I can't afford to be in this place too long, and you and I both know that they don't clean in this here hospital. I swear I saw a spider over in the corner a minute ago."

"You don't have to worry about the cost, Mama. You only need to worry about getting better. You need rest. I'm sure that spider just trying to get his rest too."

"Child, please. I'll sleep when my eyes close for good. Go get my clothes and tell them doctors to check me out. I got to go and feed my fish, I know they probably done starved to death by now."

"I've been feeding them."

I stared at her.

"Stop looking at me like I'm not telling the truth or something. I fed your stupid fish every day, I knew you'd be asking about them."

"They ain't stupid."

"They aren't stupid."

"You trying to correct your mama, Honour? I said "ain't" and that's what I meant."

"Whatever."

"You can "whatever" your behind back to Chicago. I don't need you here!" I jerked my covers back and tried to lift my leg over the bed.

"Calm down, Mama, it's not that serious and you know you can't go anywhere, so you might as well lay on back down."

"My child, who you think you be talking too? I'm still the mama around here. I ain't gonna stand for no back talking."

"I'm sorry, Mama."

I stared at her in the eyes 'cause I know she lying, but I let it go and return my leg back to the bed. Truth be told, I was glad to see her. Been too long. Hadn't seen her since Jean died.

"How long they say I got to stay in here?"

"I don't know. The shift is changing so we have to wait for the doctor to come in and examine you."

I looked at my daughter, her eyes looked tired. Her hair was not as well-fixed as normal, and I could tell there was something she wasn't telling me.

"How's the salon?"

She didn't answer me, so I asked her again.

"Honour, how's the salon?"

"Let's worry about you, Mama, we can catch up on me later."

"I know what we can do later, Honour, I asked you a question, twice now."

I watched the face of my daughter. I looked at the way her shoulders dropped. There was a pain in her eyes. A deep pain. One that I had seen before. Years ago.

"I had to close the salon, Mama."

"When and why?"

"It's a long story, nothing for you to worry about."

"What happened Honour, that salon was everything to you." I could see the tears in her eyes, they ones she didn't want me to know was lurking in the background.

"It seems a few of my stylists was running some illegal scam among other things and well...things got ugly. I closed it a few weeks ago. Look, I really don't want to talk about it."

"So, how you living without the salon? What you gonna do for money?"

"My savings. I'll find another spot and re-open once things calm down."

"Child, you broke, ain't you?"

There were the tears I knew were there.

"I'm not broke Mama." She finally managed to say.

"Honour." I reached out my hand and touched her cheek. "Child, this is your mama you talking to."

"I'll be alright, really."

"Well, I reckon it be good that I got this coma thing happening, at least that gave you a reason to come see your mama. I reckon I'm gonna need you around here for a minute." When Honour didn't respond, I knew. I knew she was in trouble. I reckon it wasn't just financially. A mama can see when her child's heart ain't working right.

FIVE
Honour Blue Baker

Fooling your mother is hard. They know every hair on your head that's out of place. At least mine did. I could see her staring at me like she was looking down into the core of my soul. Trying to find out what was causing the pain in my heart.

I wish I could explain it to her.

I wish I could tell her how hard it was to come back to this place. I know she thinks it's her, that somehow I don't love her as much as I ought to. But that's not it. My life is a mess, and I can't forget the past and the ugly role this place has played in it.

This place will never be home to me, and that's not fair. Everyone woman needs a place to call home.

"What's going on with this girl they say you found in the river?" I asked as I poured myself a glass of water.

"Child, the whole town is in a frenzy about it. The biggest news in the papers, since I can't remember when."

"Does anyone know where she came from? Did you recognize her?"

"Nope, she ain't from around here."

I studied my mother's face. "What's wrong, Mama? Why you got that worried look on your face?"

"It's just strange that's all."

"I'm sure. Finding a body in the river with your fish is certainly odd."

"True, but that's not it."

"Then, what is it?"

"Here is the thing that got my bones aching..., they say they think she somehow related to the Kings. I've been trying to figure out how that be possible since I ain't ever heard of Mildred having a child or a grandchild, for that matter. I'll tell you one thing, though, that child in that water couldn't have been over fourteen or so. The Kings were such kind people."

My hands began to shake.

"You alright, child?"

"Ma'am?" I whispered.

"I say, are you alright child, you need me to ring that nasty nurse for ya?"

I took another sip of my water. "No, Mama, I'm sorry. I'm okay."

"I never understood why you didn't like them."

"Like who, Mama?"

"The Kings."

I tried not to look at her. "Let's not go down that old road again, Mama," I said as I stood up. I knew if she could have reached me, she would take me back to my childhood days of talking back and getting a good slap across the face.

My cell phone began to ring. I stared at it but refused to answer it.

"Hiding from a boyfriend?"

"There isn't one to hid from."

There was a silence that entered the room. A silence that I knew would be broken by more revelations of what my mother felt I wasn't saying.

Mama sat up and told me to come sit on the bed next to her. She grabbed my hands and placed them in her own. When her eyes hit mine, I could barely contain the truth that was beating in me to come out.

"Some women search a lifetime for the one that makes their heart run down the street butt-naked. You always were a child that preferred to keep her heart covered up. I always wondered why."

I didn't respond. I felt her hands rub my cheek.

"You remind me so much of your father. You got his mystery. I use to have to almost drain a well to get the waters of truth to flow out from the man. He could keep a secret better than anybody I'd ever met. I miss him, Honour, but I'm glad to see him in you."

I tried to smile. It was a slow smile. One smothered in a dark void that would never be filled. I missed Daddy too.

"Anywho," Mama said as she glanced toward the window. "I wish I knew how that child was actually connected to the Kings."

"What difference does it make now?" I snapped at her. I was tired. Tired of talking about them.

"Don't get sassy with me, young lady. The Kings were good folks."

"Everyone is 'good folks' to you, Mama." She shot me a nasty look. I wanted to tell her the truth. I wanted to tell her what he did to me. But I wasn't ready. I wasn't ready for that kind of exposure."

"Where you going?"

"To find your doctor."

"Good, 'cause I need to get out of this place so I can sleep in my own bed, plus, I need to find someone that can open my locket."

My eyes glanced toward it, as it sat on the little table by mama's bed. Why did it scare me so?

"Can you take it to someone for me?"

"No, and I think you should throw it away or better yet, give it to the police."

"I'll give it to them after I done opened it first."

I watched as my mother picked up the locket and slipped it into her bra.

"Mama, really?"

"What?" She asked, trying to look as innocent as she could.

"Whatever, I need to go and find your doctor."

SIX

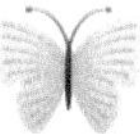

Outside mama's room, I leaned against the wall and tried to catch my breath. I hated hospitals, but, I was glad. Glad that Mama was awake.

As I walked toward the nurse's station to have the doctor paged, my cell phone began to ring again. I knew it was time.

But I was afraid.

Afraid to hear his voice.

I was also mad.

Angry.

Hurt.

But more importantly, I wanted an answer to the one question that has continued to rob me of sleep for the last couple of weeks. *Why?*

I took a deep breath and hit the answer button. "Hello."

"Honour, it's Aaron. I can't believe you finally answered your phone. You've avoided me long enough, don't you think? We need to talk."

I looked at my phone, of course, I knew it was him calling me.

I also knew that he was sitting in the office of his tax law firm, wearing a three-piece navy suit, because he loves the way a vest looks with a suit jacket, and it's Tuesday, so I knew he had just gotten out of court.

I know that he has on his Rolex, the one with the brown face on it and I know that he also has on his brown leather shoes. The ones he paid over a thousand dollars for, because to him, quality is not something he believes comes cheap.

I also know that yesterday, he arrived at the barber shop at exactly 5:05 for his haircut and the trim of his mustache that he feels no one can do just right, except the barber that he's been going to since he was in College.

In the year that we've dated, I'm come to know just about everything that a woman can know about Aaron Anthony Jones, except, why he cheated.

He was supposed to be in love with me.

I placed the phone back to my ear and wiped away the tears that were threatening to fall. "There is nothing for us to talk about Aaron."

"Please, Honour, just hear my side of the story."

"I saw your 'side' of the story, didn't I?

"Honour, I'm sorry. I've been saying those words for weeks now. I've left you messages, but you won't return my calls. I went to the salon, only to see it closed. You didn't have to close it. I know Larry told you that. He's an excellent attorney, plus the investigation the police are doing is just routine."

"Did you expect me to walk into that salon every day and not think about you. Not think about you and her? It had nothing to do with the investigation, Aaron. It had everything to do with you."

He was silent.

"I need to go. Please stop calling me." I could hear them paging mama's doctor over the intercom.

"Where are you?"

"I'm not in Chicago."

"I know, I went to your place, and one of your neighbors told me he saw you leave with a packed bag, almost a week ago. Running away is not going to solve anything, Honour. We need to talk. Face-to-face."

"I'm in Atlanta. My mother suffered a terrible fall. She was in a coma."

"Oh, baby, I'm so sorry. Why didn't you call me?"

"For what?" I started to cry.

"So I could be there. I'll leave now. I can catch a flight out and be there within a couple of hours."

"Don't bother."

"I'm coming Honour. I'll have my assistant get me a plane ticket. I'll be there in a few."

"No! I don't want you here."

"I love you, and I should be there with you, plus, I happen to believe that we deserve another chance. I'll keep saying I'm sorry until you believe that as well."

"Really?" I glanced down the corridor as the tears fell.

"Honour, you still there?"

"You know Aaron," I whispered, "you think I want your sorry excuse of an apology. I don't. I want the reason why. The reason why you did what you did. Why you hurt me."

I could tell he had leaned back in his plush office chair. I could hear the wheels moving around. He was searching. Trying to find a way not to answer me. Not to tell me the truth.

"You know what I think, Honour? I believe that you were looking for me to mess up. You were looking for a reason to run away. Yes, I was a fool to give you that reason, but baby, relationships are not made of perfect roses. Every rose has imperfections."

"Don't try to use one of your mellow-dramatic courtroom illustrations with me Aaron. I'm not one of your clients, right now. It's just me, the one who was supposed to be your girlfriend." I saw a doctor coming toward me. "You're right, roses aren't perfect, but they thrive based on how they are treated. You sleeping with a member of my staff is what's causing our relationship to wither and die. Don't call me again Aaron, you've been uprooted."

I hung up the phone before he could say another word or hear the tears that managed to hit the floor.

"Honour Blue Baker, is that you?"

Bryan Christopher Murphy came walking up toward me like he owned the very floor that his black leather shoes walked on. His creamy brown skin was just as youthful looking as it always was. Even in high school, everyone thought he was at least five years younger than he was. Hazel brown eyes and a gentle smile. The freckles were gone. The wide glasses had been replaced with contacts, and I don't remember the well-toned six-foot frame he was sporting, but it fit him rather nicely.

"Hi Bryan, long time."

"Almost twenty-three years to be exact, but who's counting."

I tried to laugh as I struggled to quickly wipe the tears away.

"You okay, Honour?"

"Yes, sorry, just got some things going on that's all."

"Anyone I need to beat up?"

We both laughed. Bryan always did have a great sense of humor. "So, you're a doctor now? The white coat looks good on you."

"I just started at this hospital, today as a matter of fact. Moved back here from Florida after my divorce."

"Oh, so sorry to hear that. How long were you married?"

"Five years."

"Any kids?"

"No, my wife, I mean my *ex-wife*, never wanted any."

"I see." I could tell talking about his ex-wife was hitting a sore spot. "I was just going to see if I could find my mother's doctor."

"I didn't know your mother was here."

"She took a nasty hit to the head and was in a coma, but she's awake now and being herself if you know what I mean?"

"Your mother was always fiery but kind."

"Fiery she still is."

. "I remember your mother's favorite words were 'ain't,' 'anywho' and 'done.' She would use them every chance she got."

I laughed. It felt good to hear it coming from me. "Those words are still her staples."

He placed his hands in his pockets as we both took a moment to remember the days when we were young. The days before things like life and adulthood stepped in.

"You look beautiful, Honour."

I didn't know how to respond to that, so I just smiled.

He reached for my hand. "Maybe later we can catch up?"

I pulled back. "You know my mother would love to see you. You know she always had a soft spot for you."

"It's a shame I never could get her daughter to feel that way."

"Wow, want happened to that shy young boy from back in the day?"

"He learned to open his mouth."

"I see."

My cell phone began to ring again.

"Boyfriend?"

"Long story."

He grabbed my hand again. "Come on, let me go say hello to your mother."

SEVEN
Emma Lee Baker

I almost wet my bed when I saw Bryan come walking into my room. I hadn't seen that boy since he was a little shrug of a thing running after Honour. Of course, my daughter never seemed to pay him no mind. Now that boy done turned into a mighty handsome doctor and I know my daughter still ain't paying the obvious, some attention. It's a doggone shame if you ask me.

"Bryan, child, you come over here and slap a hug on this ole woman. Ms. Mary told me she saw you, but I thought she was lying. Her eyesight ain't been right, in years. You probably don't even remember her, do you?"

"I remember Ms. Mary, she owned the cleaners just around the corner from the bridge."

He walked over and wrapped his arms around me. "Looks like you been working out too. You want to be my doctor?"

Bryan laughed as he walked over to pick up my medical chart. "No ma'am. But I promise that I will keep an eye on you." I caught my daughter glancing at him from the corner of the room that she managed to cozy up to.

He began looking over my medical chart. "Mrs. Baker, I see they are going to run some tests on you tomorrow."

"Child, please. You know this ole lady be fine. They only trying to run up my hospital bill, I don't need any test. How you been? How are your parents doing? I hated to see them leave here, but I know the move to Florida was good for them."

"I've been good. My parents died a few years back."

"So sorry to hear that. Your parents were good folks. I loved them dearly."

"I know. My mother always talked about that mean peach cobbler you make. You know she was mad because you never would share your recipe with her."

"Sugar, I wasn't about to share the only thing I could beat her at. Your mama could make an iron skillet sing the way my Jean could with his voice. Shoot, truth be told, your mother had my Jean running over there for her sweet potato pie every time she made it. Doggone shame."

"I remember that. Mr. Baker and my father used to sit out on the porch and fight over the last piece."

"How long are you going to be here? You back for good?"

"Yes, ma'am. I'm back for good." He glanced at Honour.

"Did you hear about that young dead girl I found floating in the water with my fish?"

"Your fish?"

Honour decided to finally come out the dark corner she'd been hiding in. "My mother has this thing with feeding the fish in the river by Thompson Mill Bridge."

"I see. That's a good walk. Good exercise too. You should keep doing that."

I shot Honour a victorious look.

"You okay, Mrs. Baker?" Bryan grabbed my arm to check my pulse. "I did hear about that young girl, but she's not dead, you know. She was just unconscious. Good thing you found her when you did."

"I know a dead body when I see one. The life of that child had done gone, I'm sure of it."

"Mrs. Baker, who's the doctor here, you or me?"

"Don't get sassy with me, doctor or not, I still can get my switch."

I thought Bryan would have laughed, but he didn't.

"Bryan, baby, you know how to open a locket?"

"Ma'am?"

Just as I went to reach for it, I felt a sharp pain shoot through me. The pain got me so bad I couldn't move. I could hear Bryan calling my name, then I see the nurses running into my room.

When I saw the look on my daughter's face, that's when I knew I was in trouble.

A few seconds later, the darkness came and tapped me on the shoulders.

EIGHT
Honour Blue Baker

I was ushered out into the hallway with nothing but a cold and worn out bench to keep me company as I watched nurses run in and out from mama's room.

Every time the door of her room opened, I'd try to scan the face I saw.

Faces.

Mama always said that a person's face can bring you hope or take away time. I admit that I never understood that until now.

For me, they took away time. Minutes seemed to have traveled to some distant land and stayed the moment the doctors went in mama's room.

With each hour that passed, I felt like I couldn't breathe. I blamed this place. I blamed this town. The people. The air. The machines that beeped continuously. I could hear them. Even through the door, I could hear the machines that were attached to my mother.

I wanted to scream. I want to cuss.

I wanted my mother to live.

She was all I had.

Finally, Bryan came out.

"What's happening? What's going on? Tell me something, Bryan. Tell me she's going to be okay."

He grabbed my hand, and I could see the agony on his face. "Your mother has slipped back into a coma. We think she might have suffered another stroke and then there's the matter of her heart. We're doing everything we can, but Honour, I'm not going to lie to you..."

"No! Don't say it. Don't you dare say it." I grabbed hold of him and clung to him. "You're going to save her, right, Bryan? Tell me you're going to save my mama."

I looked him in the eyes. Mama always said that there is a moment. A time when you can look deep into the eyes of a man and hear the words that are meant only for you.

"We're going to do all we can, Honour, I promise you that. Doctor Jacobs is one of the best here. Your mother is in good hands."

I buried my head into his chest and felt his arms wrap around me.

"Honour."

I turned around and saw Aaron standing there.

"What's going on, is your mother okay, did she...?"

I pulled away from Bryan and tried to straighten out the blouse that I was wearing. "She slipped back into a coma," I whispered.

"Oh, baby..."

I let him touch me.

I let him pull me to him.

I could smell his cologne. It was the one I brought him. The one he had worn that day. The day I...

"I came as quick as I could." Aaron looked at Bryan. "Are you her mother's doctor?"

"No, I'm Bryan. A friend of the family."

"That's right, you two grew up together. I remember Honour mentioning you... once."

Bryan looked my way.

"If she mentioned me that means I was still on her mind."

"Like I said...it was once."

I felt Aaron's arms tighten a little more around me.

Bryan reached for my hand. "Honour, you should go and try to get some rest. I'll call you right away if anything changes. You're at your mother's, right?"

"I got a room at Ms. Jaimerson's Inn, I thought that best until she came home."

"Of course. I'll call you, I promise if anything changes."

"He's right, Honour. You need to try and get some rest. I'll take you to your Hotel."

I pulled away from Aaron.

"It's okay, I can drive myself."

"Baby."

"I said, I can drive myself. Bryan, can I go in and see her first?"

"Sure."

"Do you want me to go in..."

I walked away before Aaron could finish.

NINE

Mama's wig was on crooked.

My hands began to tremble as I reached down to fix it. I remember the day I graduated from high school. She stood off to the side as my father and I made our usual jokes and gestures. She always seemed content to let him have the spotlight with me. I guess that's why she and I fussed so much. Daddy never would raise his voice at me. Mama, on the other hand, would show me what the back of her hand felt like when she needed to.

She was the one that filled my head with womanhood and what it meant to be one. She used to say..." child, keep it locked up until you be twenty-three and you can see the wedding aisle behind ya." She was the strength. She was the wisdom.

Why didn't I ever tell her? Why didn't I ever see it?

The day I left home, I almost let what happened to me, fall from my lips. I think I didn't tell her, because I was scared.

I was afraid she wouldn't believe me. Maybe it was just me. Maybe I was the one that couldn't come to grips with what had happened. I couldn't believe it. It shouldn't have been me.

I placed a kiss on her cheek and whispered in her ear.

"Mama." I stared at her eyes and squeezed her hand. "Mama, Daddy always said you were a fighter. You always thought I got my strong-willed personality from him, but I got it from you. So you fight. You fight for me, Mama. You fight for Daddy. If he were here, he'd tell you to give life a beating. I know we didn't always get along, but I love you, Mama. I love you so much, and I really need you right now. So please, Mama, please fight. I'll be back in the morning. I need to hear your voice tomorrow Mama.

"Remember how you always said that life doesn't start living inside you until you open your eyes to its possibilities? So, when I come back in the morning, I need you to open your eyes Mama and see the opportunities that exist for you and I. I'm ready now Mama. I'm ready to tell you my secret."

I cut out the light and headed toward the parking deck. I knew Aaron was probably there waiting for me.

Aaron and I stood in the hospital parking deck staring at the worn out concrete. An older couple walked by with a desperate look on their faces. I could tell they had forgotten where they had parked their car.

I could hear the lady whispering to her husband that she thought they had parked on another floor. She kept insisting that the blue signs with the white aisle numbers painted on them, didn't look familiar to her. He ignored her and tried to activate his car alarm by holding his car door opener up in the air. I heard a horn beep three times, and they rushed in that direction.

From the corner of my eye, I saw a mother trying to get her child into a car seat. There was much activity in the parking lot, and yet, none seemed to be coming from Aaron and me.

"So," Aaron said, finally breaking the barrier of silence that had built up between us, "that's the Bryan you grew up with? He didn't look exactly the way you describe him."

"What's that suppose to mean?"

"I'm just saying... I was expecting pop bottle glasses or something, and you too seemed awful..."

"We grew up together. He's my mother's doctor. Why am I even explaining this to you?"

I reached for my car door handle.

"Honour, you don't have to take everything I say as an attack."

I turned toward him. "Look, Aaron, I really think you should leave. I didn't ask you to come."

"I'm not leaving, Honour."

"Please, just go back. Go back to your..."

"Cheating life?"

"You said it, not I."

"I messed up, Honour. I admit that. I've been admitting that. But, I didn't just drop eight hundred dollars to get on a plane so I could come here and fight with you."

"You know I can give your eight hundred dollars back."

"Come on, Honour. You know that's not what I meant. I'm here because I love you. I'm in love with you."

I turned my back toward him. "Why Aaron? Why did you sleep with her?"

"Honour, look at me."

I didn't move. I wanted to hear the answer, but I didn't want to look in Aaron's eyes when he said it because I knew, I knew that if he looked back in mine, he would see how deep he had hurt me.

He stood next to me, and he leaned his back against my passenger side door. He placed his hands in his suit pockets and crossed his legs. His eyes focused on the people that continued to walk by us as he lowered his voice.

"I think I just got scared."

I turned around and leaned up against the car, next to him. We both stared at the concrete again.

"I knew that I was falling in love with you and I knew what that meant. I've been running away from the idea of marriage all my life. I think that's why we worked. We both were running from the same thing. I didn't plan what happened, I swear to you."

He tried to grab my hand, but I pulled away. "I caught the two of you in my office. In my office! My staff knew what was going on the moment I walked in the salon that day. How could you Aaron? How could you do that to me... to us?"

"Honour, I know I will be apologizing for that forever, but I want to marry you. I don't want to live my life without you. I know you love me, baby. Look at me. I'll do anything. Anything."

He moved in front of me and gently pulled me to him. I could feel my body responding to his touch, as our eyes locked in on each other. The beating of my heart, I was sure could be heard throughout the parking deck as he leaned in.

"Stop it. We're in the hospital's parking lot. People are starting to stare."

"I don't care." His voice softened. "Please, Honour, forgive me. I'm nothing without you. I want to marry you."

My mind kept saying...fight, don't give in, but my heart kept saying...why? "Aaron, please." I eased myself out of his embrace.

"Look, I'm not going to play that game by telling you that she meant nothing to me. She was something, just not in the way you imagine. She was a way to be the old me, not the me, that fell in love with you. She gave me comfort in an old space that I use to dwell in. A space that allowed me to act as if my heart wasn't beating for you. I'm going to tell you something even though the man inside begs me not to." He paused for a moment. "I think I wanted you to find us."

"Really, Aaron?"

"Yes, really. I think I knew that's the only way I would stop. The only way I would face up to the reality that the old me was done."

"I don't believe that."

"That's fair, but what I say is true. Think about it, I knew when you arrived at the shop. In fact, since we're speaking the truth here, I heard you come in, but I didn't move from her, even when I heard you at the door. It was as if my body said, take it. That I deserved the look, you were going to give me. I deserved to see the pain I had caused. That's why I didn't run and I didn't coward out. The most realist thing I can say to you is that the moment I saw your face, was the moment that I realized just how much I no longer wanted that life. I wanted you."

He came into my intimate space again. I could smell my fear. The fear of him touching me. The fear of me not moving away. When he placed his lips on mine, I felt my heart slow down. His lips felt like....

"Stop it, Aaron! Just...stop. Please. Go home." I tried to stop the tears from coming. I fought them with all that I had, but the war was lost the moment I looked him in the eyes and knew. I knew that I would never get that image out of my head. I knew the fear would never leave me. The fear that he would do it again...

...Hurt me.

I pushed him away.

"You can't forgive me, Honour?"

His hands reached for my cheek. I couldn't look at him. I couldn't allow him to draw me in. I wanted to scream. I wanted to run away, but most of all, I wanted to deny how much I loved him.

My mother was a believer in love. She believed it never failed. So why? Why did I feel like it had failed me?

"Honour Blue Baker, our relationship is worth fighting for. I'm here Honour. I'm fighting. I'm fighting for the life we can have. For the future we want. I'm fighting for your forgiveness. I'm fighting for your heart. I'm fighting for your love. Baby, I love you." He placed his hands in his pocket and pulled out a box.

The one everyone woman dreams of.

The velvet one.

As he got down on one knee, I felt my legs begin to wobble.

"I need you, Honour Blue Baker. Will you be my wife?" He opened it slowly. "You will never find another man who will love you like me."

Like me. Aaron's words rang in my head. Circled around my emotions and answered my question. The journey seemed to take forever. The struggle was all too real, but my conclusion was simple.

Love didn't fail me. He did.

I took a deep breath, reached out and closed the box.

"You're right, Aaron. No other man will ever love me the way you do."

"Are you saying, yes?"

"Let me finish. You see, no other man will ever love me with pain attached to it. They will never love me with hurt lingering in the background. Neither will they touch me the way you did. Their touch will be filled with trust. Their fingers will linger on my skin with respect for our relationship. Their lips will embrace mine with a passion for honesty and when they hold me, I will know that they only belong to me. So, you're right, they will not be like you."

"Honour, you know I didn't mean it like that."

"Perhaps, but that's my truth. That's the truth that I hear when I look at you. Go home, Aaron."

"Here," he placed the box in my hand. "I'm not giving up."

"Did you hear what I just said, Aaron?"

"Yes, I heard you. I heard that I have to prove that you can trust me again. I heard that I must show that you can love me past the pain I've caused. I heard that I have to make it so that when I touch you, you want to touch me back."

As he stroked the side of my cheek. I could feel the warmth of his fingers.

"I heard that I have to prove that you belong to me. So yes, I heard you."

I watched him walk towards his rental car, my mind kept telling me that I had made the right decision, but my heart wanted to slide that ring on my finger and allow him to change my last name.

Love.

It was not giving up.

I climbed into my car and started the engine.

TEN

My hands shook as I turned the steering wheel.

Even in the darkness, I could find it.

It's funny how we go back to the things that hurt us the most. As if, standing in the shoes of our past would fit better now that we're older and know how to tie the strings of life up in a neat little bow.

One more turn to the right.

One more turn and I'll be tripping over the source of my nightmares.

The moment the street came into view, I felt my heart pick up the pace. My throat felt like it was closing in on me. The sweat of anxiety began to build up and make a neat little home over my upper lip. I gripped the steering wheel as I passed by one white fenced home after another, until I reached the last one.

The big one.

The one with the unpleasant memories locked behind an old stained door.

The big oak tree was still there. The grass, although uncut, was still green. The windows were boarded. The white paint that once dressed the house had dulled and now resembled nothing but hues of dark gray. Cobwebs wrapped their arms around it.

The rocking chair that Mildred King used to brag was given to them by John F. Kennedy was gone. It was made out of green wood and crafted by the P & P Chair Company, as she often stated.

As I got out of the car and stood against it, I could hear the crickets screaming.

Where were they twenty-three years ago, when I needed them to be my voice. To say the things that I was afraid to say....That the man who lived in this house, raped me.

The man that always had the friendly smile.

The man that helped my father get decent wages for his singing when some didn't want to pay him his worth.

The man that my mama called Paul instead of Mr. King like everyone else.

I remember when the humiliation was almost over, he said to me, "Don't forget to grab that peppermint out of the dresser drawer and give it to your mama, and if you want your daddy to continue working in this town, you'll keep your mouth shut."

Those words.

Those words sealed the deal. My humiliation was complete.

I had just turned eighteen.

Four months later, I was in Chicago.

Facing college.

Facing motherhood.

A decision had to be made.

PART TWO
L'orraine

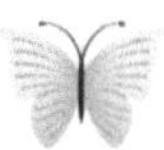

ELEVEN

Ella and I hid in our rooms like two young girls playing hide and seek. Only there wasn't a real place to hide. Nothing but two beds, a single nightstand and a small lamp that barely stayed lit. The white starched walls of our bedroom terrorized us. The thin pieces of material that once resemble blue drapes blew like crazy because the window was slightly cracked.

I'd left the windows open on purpose. I was convinced that young girls wouldn't grow without the wind on their skin.

"Do you hear that, Sister?" Ella asked.

I'd heard it. The booming sound of thunder just over our heads.

"It's too close," she whispered.

"We'll be alright, I promised. I won't let the lightning get you. I'll always be here to protect you." I reached over and gave her a gentle pinch.

We both laughed.

"One day Sister, you're going to leave me. You can't stay here forever. You're twenty-three-years-old, and you're the only mama I've known."

I could see the tears in her eyes.

"No I'm not, besides, you've got Old Big Bones."

Her laughter was a peaceful touch that tickled down to my

bones. A gentle tap upon my heart. It came as quickly as it could have and left just as suddenly.

That's what her voice did for us. Stole the laughter away. Took the joy out of our smiles and left us bare as a child's bottom.

"Lorraine, you get your butt down here now! Right now! You hear me?"

"You'd better go," Ella whispered. I could see the fear on her face.

"I'm tired of her beating on us. It isn't right."

"I know, but, Daddy doesn't seem too. You had better go on, you know she will only get madder if you take too long."

"I don't care," I boldly whispered. "Besides, I'm a grown woman. It's time for us to stand up to Old Big Bones.

"You might be grown, but, her switch apparently doesn't think so."

We laughed again. A little lower than before.

The door to our shared bedroom flung open and Old Big Bones stood towering over us with a switch in her hands.

"Something the matter with your ears, girl?"

I gave her a smile.

"Something funny?"

I still didn't open my mouth. I just kept smiling. I knew it was going to cost me, but I was willing to pay the price. Something inside me was roaring like a lion. Something fierce was boiling in my blood, and no matter how long or wide she swung that switch, my insides weren't going to shut up.

"You better answer me!" She raised her hand and allowed the switch to dangle in my face.

I didn't flinch. Even as the switch rocked softly in the air, I kept my smile plastered on my face.

"You must like a good beating."

"Leave her alone!" Ella shouted.

She flipped her neck and shot my younger sister a look.

I watched as Old Big Bones moved from in front of me and toward Ella. The switch swung high in the air. I could see the fear in Ella's eyes as she turned around to block the impending attack from hitting her in the face. My rage began to travel up through my nostrils. Fire filled the corners of my eyes.

The first slash hit Ella right in the center of her back, and she screamed. It echoed in my mind, raced down to my toes and caused my legs to move.

I charged at Old Big Bones.

"Ella, get out, get out now, Ella!" I screamed as I grabbed hold of the solid hand that had its grip around the switch. I could feel her trying to break free from my hold, but I didn't let go.

Out the corner of my eye, I saw Ella scramble out the room.

Old Big bones reached out with her other hand and grabbed hold of me and flung me across the room. I quickly gathered to my feet. I wanted her to know that I wasn't afraid. That I wasn't backing down.

I closed my hands into mighty fists and braced my feet. "You aren't beating on us anymore!"

The corners of her thick lips formed into a chuckle. "Well now, you finally got some courage in them bones. It only took you twenty-three years, but it isn't going to save you!"

The switch flew into the air again. You could hear it. It came down toward me with a fierceness and quickness I'd never seen before, but I reached out and grabbed hold of it, just before the tip of its leather got hold of my skin. I gripped it hard and pulled with every ounce of strength my body could find. It freed from her ugly fingers, and I threw it across the room.

We stood face-to-face. One raging bull to another. Neither of us ready to back down. Then I smiled again.

"What's going on in here?" Daddy stood in the doorway. His forty-five years of working as a janitor at the hospital was showing on his face. It was the only thing he knew how to do—besides, drink.

Old Big Bones stepped back from me as he came further into the room. "I'm tired of these here girls!" She pointed her fat little finger towards me. "They ain't listening to me. You just let them do whatever they want in this house. I'm tired, Charles! Plus, this one here is too grown to even be in this house. Her butt should have been out of here a long time ago. You know I'm right Charles!"

"Fine, but what are you beating them for?"

She turned slowly toward him. "I was downstairs, she heard me calling her, and she didn't come. Made me walk all the way up here."

I watched as my father's eyes darted from me to her. "That's no reason to be beating on them like this. No more. You understand me, Clarisse?"

Clarisse. Ella and I had been calling her Old Big Bones for so long, I had forgotten she had a first name.

"You aren't going to tell me how to discipline these girls, Charles!"

"Lorraine is not a child, Clarisse. She's a grown woman. She doesn't need you to discipline her."

"So you admit that she needs to get out? If she ain't going to listen and you don't want me disciplining her, then, she needs to leave. We can't have two grown women in this house!"

"Clarisse, I'm going to tell you this, and I want you to listen real good to what I'm going to say because I'm tired. I've been working all day, and I got to go back tonight for a few hours. Now, I know I have been drunk for most of the time you've been here, but I haven't't' had one drink today and don't plan to ever drink again." He glanced in my direction. "Now, you put your hands on my girls again, and I'll put you out." He turned and left the room before she could respond.

Daddy's words traveled down to my kidneys and gave them a warm hug. I felt like I had been waiting my whole life to hear them.

TWELVE

About an hour later, the rain outside had finally stopped, and the moon took its stand. Ella slowly came into the room as I lay in my bed. Her shoulder length blond hair was damp, and I could see the tears in her big green eyes. Her slightly rounded cheeks were red, and her slim frame moved in pain.

She walked over toward the closet and pulled out a shirt. I could see the mark the switch had left as she changed into it.

"I'm sorry," I said as I began to tell her what had happened.

"I can't believe Daddy finally stood up to Old Big Bones." She said as she eased down onto her bed.

"Yes, the pigs must be flying on the clouds outside."

She laughed. "I did see them as I was running to hide in the mud they love so much."

I sat up when she suddenly got quiet.

"I thought she was going to kill you, Lorraine. I really did." I saw the tears forming in the corners of her eyes again.

Ella never called me by my real name, unless she was scared. I tapped the edge of my bed, and she came and sat down next to me. I placed my arm around her shoulder and pulled her close. "I wasn't going to let that happen without a fight, I promise you that."

She looked up at me. "You know she isn't going to stop. Daddy isn't here most of the time. She'll find a way to get us. It might not be by that switch, but I know she'll find a way."

Her tears began to fall slowly now. I tried to wipe them away like our mama used to do when Ella was just a baby.

Ella looks just like her.

"Sister?"

"Yes, Ella."

"You sing to me? You used to do it all the time."

"You're too big for that now. Besides, you need to try and go to sleep."

"Please, Lorraine."

She curled up in my arms. I wrapped them around her tightly and stroked her hair as I sang.

"I could listen to you sing forever, Sister. I wish you would do it more often."

"Go to sleep."

She buried her head in my chest and closed her eyes.

As I sang, I thought of her.

Our real mother.

Her name was Barbara Chambers

Memories of her are vague at times, but when I close my eyes and allow my mind to clear away all the bad stuff, I see her.

I remember her favorite things.

Butterflies.

She loved them.

She loved the vibrant colors of their opened wings. She loved to watch them dance on a flower. Especially the red ones. She said they reminded her of something special.

Love.

My mother had slightly round and rosy cheeks. Big green eyes and long blond hair. There was always a smile on her face and a heart the size of the world. Daddy also said that her beauty could be seen in the wings of a butterfly.

It was a butterfly that brought my parents together. The day my father met my mother, she had one in her hand. She said to him, *"Isn't the color of this butterfly just beautiful? It's called a Painted-Lady. Come take a look. It has red wings."*

He had looked into her hand and then into her eyes. That's all it took.

THIRTEEN

My mother died when I was thirteen from cancer. Ella was around four then. Daddy had just walked into the house after pulling a double shift, to pick us up and take us to see her. By then, she was in a place that you go to when there is nothing else the doctors can do for you.

I heard my father once call it hospice.

The night of my mother's funeral, after everyone had left, Daddy sat at the kitchen table and drank until he could barely stand. He did that for a week. Then one day he came home from work and told us to go over to the neighbor's house. We didn't see him for a month after that. When he did came back, you would have sworn a different man walked into the doorway.

For that point on, the bottle seemed to never leave his hand.

Two years later, Old Big Bones came into our home with her loud mouth and bad cooking. I knew Daddy didn't love her. He barely looked at her. He barely looked at Ella and I, for that matter.

It was two in the morning when the door of our bedroom flew open. The impact of its cold sting felt like daggers upon my skin. She held the water hose in her hands. Her laugh bounced off the walls as she aimed it at me. I felt like I was drowning as I grabbed hold of my one-bed sheet and tried to wrap it around me.

"Stop it! Stop it, please!" Ella shouted.

"Shut up, child, or you'll be next!"

"You're drowning her!"

"I said shut up!" She turned the water hose towards Ella, but as soon as I went to move, she immediately swung it back around and used its full force to contain me.

"Please stop!" I cried. The water filled my ears. It went deep into my nose, my mouth, and caused my insides to feel as if they were floating. I cried out again, "Please Clarisse. Please stop."

Finally, she turned the water off and stood there, looking at me with a smile on her face.

"Why?" Is all I could mutter.

She walked over to my bed and whispered in my ear, The foulness of her breath traveled up my nostrils. "You think I don't know what you and that brat call me? But, that's not why I hate you." She leaned in more. "I hate you because you're a Negro. Your daddy ain't man enough to tell you the truth. Your mama was one. Your real mother that is. She gave you up, and his sorry behind took you in."

"You're lying!"

"Am I? Ask him, he'll tell you that I'm telling the truth. You're a no good little Black girl all dressed up in a white woman's body. But your insides don't lie. Look in the mirror."

She grabbed me by the throat. "I bet right now, you want to hurt me. I can see it in your eyes. I bet you want to run to your weak daddy, but if you even think about telling him about our little water hose episode, I'll kill Ella, she's not your sister anyway." She released me. "I want you out of this house." She walked toward the door, picked up the hose and dragged it with her. "You got until dinner time to get out."

When she closed our bedroom door, she took the world I had known, with her.

Ella ran over to me. "Lorraine, you alright?"

I wrapped my arms around my body and curled up in my wet bed.

"Lorraine, what did she say? What did she whisper in your ear?"

"Go back to bed, Ella."

"Lorraine."

"Please, Ella, go back to bed."

I listened for the squeak of her bed. When I knew she was under the covers, I let them fall.

One tear after the next.

I waited until I knew Ella was deep asleep before I climbed from my bed. Even in the early morning moonlight, I could see myself in the mirror.

My long, wavy golden blond hair hung around my neck, dripping in water.

Daddy's hair is golden blond.

Daddy's eyes are Hazel.

My eyes are Hazel.

I touched my skin.

I looked at my hands.

I pulled off my wet nightgown.

I stared.

I stared at every crevice. Every curve.

I was convinced of one thing— I was white.

FOURTEEN

I heard daddy come in.

I listened to his footsteps. I knew after he took off his work boots he would head for the kitchen.

He always did. That's where the liquor was.

I moved as quietly around the room as I could, slipping on a pair of jeans, gym shoes and a sweatshirt. I pulled my wet hair back into a ponytail and headed toward the door. The floors squeaked as I reached for the door knob.

"Where are you going?" Ella asked.

"Go back to sleep. It's not time for you to get up yet."

I waited until she placed her head upon her pillow and closed her eyes before I eased out of the room.

As I crept down the hallway, I could hear him opening the kitchen cabinet. The one over the refrigerator. The one that held a bottle of Jack Daniels.

He was reaching for a glass as I walked in.

"Lorraine! Don't be sneaking up on me like that."

"I thought you said you weren't going to drink anymore."

"It was a rough night. Folks at that hospital have no respect for a janitor. What are you doing up? It's five o'clock. You don't have to get Ella up for camp for another hour."

"Daddy, I need to ask you something. Something important."

"It can't wait until later?"

"No, sir."

He walked over toward the kitchen table. Placed his glass and his bottle of Jack Daniels on it and took a seat.

My knees shook. My throat felt dry and I could feel the bubbles of sweat forming on my upper lip. I braced my body against the kitchen chair. My hands gripping the chair like my life depended on it.

"Girl, what is going on with you?"

When I opened my mouth, I knew my lips were moving, but I couldn't hear any sound coming from them. The sound of the question that I needed the answer to...

"Am I a...a Negro?" I whispered.

"What did you say? Speak up, Lorraine, I can't hear you."

I cleared my throat and gripped the chair even harder.

"I said, Am I a Negro?"

"Don't' you ever use that word in this house. You hear me!"

My eyes didn't blink at his anger. I knew the consequences would be severe. I knew my heart would stop, but I had to know. I had to know if there was depth to the claim of Old Big Bones.

"Am I, Daddy? Am I black?"

"Who told you that?"

"Was my real mother...was she black?"

I watched as he poured his drink. His hands shook. But it was his eyes. It was his eyes that confirmed it.

Silence came into the kitchen. It was like someone had opened the window and it just flew in and made itself a home.

He poured another drink, and I watched his throat move.

"Daddy please."

"I can't." He whispered.

"I have to know."

"Your mother is dead. Barbara, the woman that loved you. She died ten years ago from cancer. That's all you need to know. That's all that really matters."

I watched as the tears flowed down his cheeks.

It was the second time I had seen him cry.

I sat down, and as I reached over and laid my hand upon his, I looked at the lines of his face. The gentleness that once existed when I was a little girl had come back to me. This was the daddy I had grown up with. This was the daddy that my heart had loved for twenty-three years.

"Yes, Daddy, you're right," I murmured, "she will always be my mother, but was she the woman that gave birth to me?"

He stared at my hand. His countenance dropped.

"It's okay Daddy, you can tell me. You can tell me the truth. Was she the woman that gave birth to me?"

The answer that would rock my entire world slipped off his lips. It wasn't easy for him to say it and it was even harder for me to accept. But finally, it was there. It bounced off the kitchen walls and landed between us.

"No. No, she wasn't."

I leaned back. My hand no longer touching his. I let those words slip down my bones. They touched me in ways that pain has never dared before.

Drops of tears splashed upon the table.

From both of us.

"Do not hate us for not telling you."

Hate. That was a word I never thought I would consider. A feeling I never imagined I would have for anyone other than ole big bones.

"Did she not love me? Is that why she gave me up? Was I too... too white for her?"

He stared at this glass. That burning desire to once again suffocate his pain with a liquid he imagined could do the job, was taking control of him.

"You can't run away, Daddy. Not this time. You can't hide from the pain. You can't throw all your sorrows into the bottom of a bottle, and you can't stop the truth from being what it is. I need to know. Please."

He raised his glass to his lips, but then stopped and placed it back on the table.

"You weren't the reason why she gave you up."

"Then what was the reason? What reason could she possibly

have had, that would warrant this moment? This moment that would destroy a life that I have believed to be real and now is not?"

"It was the memories."

"The memories?"

"The memories of being raped by a white man. She told us his first name, but now all I can remember is that his last name was King. He had been a friend of the family. Someone she had grown up knowing and trusted."

He got up from the table. "I can't do this. Barbara and I promised her we would never..."

"Please Daddy, my childhood fairytale has already been lost. We both have to face the ugliness that I must now call reality...

I am black."

He sat back down and placed his hand upon mine. It was the first time that I saw the difference.

"Being black is not ugliness Lorraine. It is beautiful. Do you remember the thing Barbara adored the most?"

I began to sob.

"It was butterflies. She loved them. Their colors were their beauty. They each have more than one and yet people still only called them butterflies. You are no different. Your wings are outlined in white, but it is your core color that makes you radiant."

"The world does not believe in butterflies, Daddy."

"It doesn't matter what the world believes, it only matters what you believe. Do you believe in butterflies Lorraine?"

I had said early that she would always be my mother. The woman with the soft smile and happy heart. The woman who gave me life even though she didn't bring me into it. I couldn't let her memory fly away as if it never existed. Her memory was all that I had to hold on to. Everyone must believe in something real.

"Yes Daddy, I believe in butterflies."

His hand left mine as he placed the cap on the Jack Daniels and leaned back in his chair.

"Daddy, I have to ask...."

His eyes meant mine again.

"Do you know my birth mother's name?"

He slowly nodded his head.

"Is she still alive?"

"I don't know. We had an adoption agency take care of everything for us, just in case."

"Just in case, what?

"Just in case she tried to change her mind or tried to..."

"Contact me?"

"Yes."

"What is her name?"

"Her name was Honour. Honour Blue Baker."

FIFTEEN

"We met her at the hospital."

"She and Barbara shared a hospital room. They got pretty close, and Honour confided in Barbara, she told her everything. She was from some county just outside of Atlanta, called Barrow. Her parents thought she was coming to Chicago to go to college. They had no idea she was four months pregnant when she left.

"She was so young. Only eighteen at the time.

"Everything that happened that day we met her, everything that was said or done, was unbelievable. I don't know how to explain it, except to say that, on that day lives changed in ways no one in that room could imagine.

"Honour was moments away from getting ready to bring life into the world and I was moments away from hearing the news that would evidently take the life of my wife away. "

He stared off. I could tell he was back there. Sitting in the hospital room, holding her hand.

"Barbara, you have cancer," the doctor stated so plainly. "It's stage four, and given this is your fourth miscarriage we are going to have to advise you against any immediate efforts to get pregnant."

"But, I can get pregnant?"

"Baby, did you hear the doctor? You have cancer."

"If I'm going to die, I'm going to give you something to remember me by."

"Daddy." I reached over and touched his hand.

His eyes blinked. "Barbara was such a strong woman. I've never loved another woman as much as I loved her...and I doubt I ever will." He glanced at the Jack Daniels bottle again. "If she saw me now..."

"She would forgive you."

"For some of it, yes. She was that kind of woman." He stood up. "The adoption was Barbara's idea." I watched as he walked over toward the cabinet, the one above the refrigerator, and pulled out a small wooden box. "I never intended to give you this." He placed his hand on top of the box. "Maybe that was wrong, but I never wanted you to believe you were anything other than our daughter." He placed the box on the table in front of me and returned to his seat.

Fear is something that stops time. It stops movement. It lingers on the outskirts of our past and traces the lines of our future. We're afraid to breathe it in and yet it consumes us. We try to deny its existence. We cuss at it and run from it, but in the end, it slams us in the face and demands that we acknowledge its grip on our moments. Our moments in life when we must face it.

As I traced the edge of the box with my fingers, the tears began to fall again. I closed my eyes for a few seconds and took a deep breath. I could hear my heart pounding and my legs shaking.

At twenty-three, I had not learned how to come off victorious after battling with fear.

"It okay," my father said. "Open it."

I pulled out a tarnished gold locket and a key.

"About a year after you were born, we got an envelope in the mail from the adoption agency. It seems the nurses at the hospital you were born in, made a tradition out of taking pictures of the new mothers holding their children for the first time. They took a picture of Honour holding you. The adoption agency forwarded the picture to us. We placed it in that locket. The locket belonged to Barbara's father. He gave it to her on our wedding day. It was her 'something old'. It's been in her family for over a century. It requires the key to open it."

I saw the tears building back up in his eyes. "I want you to know that the moment Barbara and I looked at you, we loved you, and it wasn't because you looked white. It was because you were ours.

"When you came into our lives, you gave us both something worth fighting for. You were the reason Barbara stayed alive as long as she did. You gave her ten years of loving a child she never thought she would have. Even when we finally had Ella, she never saw you as anything other than her own. I have never seen you as anything other than my own. You have to know Lorraine, you have to believe how much we loved you and..." He placed his hands over his face. The tears came fast and hard as he broke down.

I placed the locket and the key on the table and ran to my father. I wrapped my arms around him and buried my tears in his pain.

"It's okay daddy. It's okay. I know you love me. I know mama loved me."

"I miss her so much Lorraine that I started to hate her. I began to hate her for leaving me. For leaving us." He wrapped his arms around me and help me tight.

"I miss her too, daddy. I really do."

SIXTEEN

"You're not my real sister?"

Neither of us had noticed. Neither of us had seen her come in, but there Ella stood with her eyes filled with tears and holding the locket.

"Ella, I will always be your sister."

"No, you're going to leave me now. I heard you two. I heard everything."

I tried to go to her, but she held her hand out to keep me from coming near. "You're going to go off to your real family and leave me here with Old Big Bones and a daddy who could care less!"

She held the locket in the air.

"No, Ella, that's not true. Please give me the locket."

"Yes, it is! You're lying! You're going to leave me." She looked at my father as she gripped the locket in her hand. "I hate you! All you do is drink, and now you're taking the one person that really loves me!" She ran from the kitchen. We heard the front door open and then slam shut.

"I will go find her," I whispered.

"No, she needs me. She needs me to finally be what I haven't been in a long time...A father."

"You and your sister had better stop all that screaming this early in the morning!" Old Big Bones stated as she walked into the kitchen pretending like she didn't know what was going on.

Daddy gave her a very nasty look as he began to walk out of the kitchen.

"Where are you going?"

"To put my boots on and find Ella."

"She's just spoiled. Looking for attention, if you ask me. I'd let her stay out there for awhile. Teach her a lesson."

"I'm sure you would."

"What's that suppose to mean?"

"It means that when I get back, you and I are going to have a good chat."

"Go find your little-spoiled brat Charles. I don't have time for no chat this morning, I have to get my breakfast on. You want me to put the Jack Daniels back in the cabinet or are you still working on it?" She gave him a sinister smile.

Daddy glared at her as he left the kitchen.

She waited until she heard the front door open and close before she moved towards me, grabbing me by the arm.

"I meant what I said. I want you out of this house."

"I'm not going anywhere!" I spat back at her.

"Oh, dear child, you most certainly are. In fact, I've changed my mind, I want you gone before your daddy walks back in this house or else."

"I'm not afraid of you."

"Yes, you are. I can feel the fear running through your veins. If you don't get your butt out of this house before he comes back, I won't turn that water hose off the next time. I'll drown your black behind!"

I tried to snatch myself away from her, but her grip was too tight. She swung me around and slammed me up against the refrigerator.

"You can try to act brave if you want too, but you had better not try me!"

She wrapped her hands around my neck, lifting my feet off the floor. "You will leave right now, won't you? Nod your head."

I nodded my head.

"Good." She released her hold on me.

I grabbed my neck and tried to catch my breath as I leaned up against the refrigerator. "I...I need some money. If you want me out of this house so bad, then I need some money."

She glared at me and then moved toward the bottom kitchen cabinet. Reached in the back and pulled out a jar filled with money.

"I knew this day would come," she said as she threw the jar at me. "There's a thousand dollars or so in there, maybe a little more. It's more than enough to get you a one-way bus ticket out of Chicago."

"You'll leave Ella alone if I go?" I asked, as I took the money out of the jar and placed it in my pocket. Keeping one eye on her at all times.

"As long as you stay gone, I won't touch a hair on her spoiled white head."

"What am I supposed to do about clothes?"

"You're wearing some, aren't you?"

Her eyes followed my gaze toward the table. The key to the locket lay just in front of the opened box.

We both moved toward it.

It wasn't just a key. It was a key to a locket that I may never get a chance to see the inside of, but it was all I had left, and I wasn't leaving without it.

SEVENTEEN

It took four buses.

Four buses to arrive at a place that would take me from my past and dump off into a future that I wasn't sure I was ready for.

As the entrance to Greyhound Bus Station stood just a few feet from me, I clutched the key in my left hand and tried to fight back the tears that threatened to remind me that I had nothing. Nothing but the clothes on my back and the shoes on my feet.

Once inside, my knees shook. I searched faces, and no one noticed, except a woman. She was older. I put her around fifty or so. Her slightly bronzed skin was smooth, and her smile was kind. She had three pieces of luggage with a designer name on them, staged rather neatly by her side. Her legs were crossed with a five-inch heel slightly tilted into the air. She spoke rapidly on her cell phone but glanced in my direction to acknowledge my existence. The look took no more than a second, but it gave me what I needed.

The courage to move although slowly, toward the ticketing window.

The lady behind it barely looked up. "Where are you headed?" She asked. I stood there begging my lips to move. Longing for my throat to utter a sound. A sound that suggested that I had a particular direction.

"Either tell me where you're headed or I'm going to have to ask you to step aside." She barked at me. I could feel the tension of the people that had gathered in line behind me.

The ones that knew where they were headed.

"Atlanta," I finally whispered, "I need a one-way ticket to Atlanta."

A few seconds later the ticket was thrust into the silver window tray, which she pushed out into my direction. "How many pieces of luggage?"

"Ma'am?"

"I said, how many pieces of luggage do you need to check in?"

"None," I replied as I lowered my head. "I don't have any luggage."

"The bus to Atlanta is leaving in thirty minutes... Next."

The man behind me almost pushed me out of the way.

'Next.' It was such a simple word. For me, it meant leaving Ella.

My feet wanted to go back as I climbed the stairs of the bus. Faces of people that I would spend the next 18 hours or so stared at me as I searched for an empty seat. I found one next to the older lady I had seen earlier.

A few minutes later, the bus driver closed the door, and when I felt the bus pulling out, I closed my eyes to keep from screaming.

EIGHTEEN

The oak trees of Chicago could be barely seen as we made our way. The rooftops of homes I had seen all my life, would soon no longer be a part of my life.

The 'L' traveled up the center of the Dan Ryan Expressway. Packed with people. Hundreds of cars flew by. In my attempt to pass the time, I had tried to count them, but as the hours ticked away, I gave up.

I watched as grocery stores, gas stations, and familiar streets faded into the mid-afternoon sun. I placed my hand on the window as the 'Thank You For Visiting Chicago' sign came into view.

I said good-bye to her. To Ella.

"You want the window seat?"

"No ma'am."

"Here, let's switch. I like the aisle seat and most younger people like the window since they don't have to go to the bathroom as much."

She stood up before I could protest further. "It looks like you have an admirer." She said as we made the awkward seat exchange.

"Ma'am?"

"That young man a few rolls up on the left. He's been staring at you for the last five hours. Tries to act like he's not, but I see him." I looked up a few rolls. When our eyes met, he looked away.

"He's cute. He may be a bit older than you, I suspect, but a few years don't hurt anybody. Don't you agree?"

"I don't know. I guess."

"Of course, he's mighty bold seeing that I'm sitting here. As your pretend mother, I could go over and give him a slap upside the head for checking out my pretend daughter. I guess that's the world we living in now. A world of boldness."

She winked at me.

"My only daughter allowed the boldness of the world to infect her thinking. She up and married a white man. Of course, I didn't approve at first. Didn't think it was right, but, he turned out to be a good man so I had to stop complaining about him to her face. Don't get me wrong, I don't hate white people, I wouldn't be talking to you if I did, but I never expected my child to run off and marry one. She said it was for love. How she knows anything about love, I don't know, and besides, we had only been in New York for a few weeks on business. When they met, he was working in a coffee shop. I will admit he's smart. He's supposed to be going to law school next year. I'm glad, at least one day, he'll have his own money. I just hope it comes before they start popping out my grandchildren.

"I wanted my daughter to sign one of those forms, you know... a prenup, but she nearly laughed in my face when I suggested the idea. I tried to tell her that one can never be too careful. My daughter is young. I wish she would have waited until she was older before she got married. Shoot, I was a mere twenty-one year old when I met my husband, so I tried to talk to her from experience, but young women always think that us older women are just naive to the ways of the world. She doesn't understand that it was us older women that built the world she living in."

I stared at her.

"Too much information? I know. I have always been that way. My late husband always said that whenever I walked away from a conversation, I left butt-naked. He had a good sense of humor, and that was about it. I gave him twenty-nine years of my life. He died three days ago. He was hit by a car just as he was leaving his girlfriend's home. I guess the good Lord wanted to spare me going to prison.

"The bimbo he was seeing, lives in Atlanta. He always claimed he was going there for business. Now, I know that was a lie. I'm on my way to bring him back to Chicago for the funeral my daughter is trying to convince me to have. I told her that I could put him in the dirt, six feet deep, all by myself. Of course, I wouldn't have killed him myself, I'd would have just hired someone." She looked me in the eye and began to laugh. "You thought I was serious didn't you?"

I shook my head yes.

"Good. I was. I bet you hate I made you take the window seat now. You can't run away."

I shook my head in agreement.

She began to laugh a little louder this time.

"You're an honest young thing, aren't you. Good, I love honesty. Don't worry, I don't mean any harm, it's just the bitterness talking. What's your name?"

"Lorraine Thomas."

"Lorraine, that's a lovely name. My aunt was named Lorraine. I hated that woman."

I searched for an empty seat.

"Relax, I was joking that time. My aunt was named Lorraine, but she was a beautiful woman who would give you the shirt off her back if she thought you needed it."

She reached out her hand. "My name is Dena. Dena Fox, but most just call me Mrs. D."

I tried to smile as I shook her hand.

"You don't talk much do you or is it that I haven't really given you a chance too?"

Before I could answer, she started talking again.

"I'm sorry, I don't know why I'm even asking that. I do talk too much. It's inherited, I think. I bet I could talk the socks off a cold man." She crossed her legs and sat up in her seat. "I bet my husband's girlfriend was the silent type. I bet she's probably about your age knowing him. I'm tempted to find out, once I get there, but I'm not sure if I have the nerves to carry it through. I feel like I'm at war with my fear of seeing her and my fear of killing her if I do see her." She leaned back in her seat. "It's always hard to box with fear, especially when you aren't sure how the fight will turn out. You know what I mean?"

I nodded. I really did know what she meant.

She smiled. "You're probably wondering why I got this fur coat on in the dead of summer. Well, I figure that if I do see her, I need to look good. I need to let her know where the money came from that he spent on her. I got my best pair of heels on. My pearl necklace and my most expensive pair of diamond earrings on. Of course, if I need to whoop that tail, I'll take my diamond earrings off."

She touched her ear. "These are just too cute to get messed up while handling your business. I wasn't always rich you see. I grew up on the low-income streets of Chicago. The Hood, if truth be told. I made my money the hard way. Worked my butt off for every penny and he went and spent some of my hard-owned money on her. Makes me what to wake him up from the deep sleep of death and slap the black off him! He ain't got much by the way. He had a lot of cream in his skin if you know what I mean. But I'd slap him so hard, I'd find the real black in him. That I promise you."

She glanced out the window next to me and sighed.

"So, if you're rich, then why are you riding the Greyhound?"

She laughed. Loudly.

"Sorry, I needed that laugh. Girl, I believe in staying rich. My daughter says I'm cheap. I call it not forgetting where you come from."

She glanced up at the boy that had been staring at me and winked. He quickly turned back around in his seat.

"Truth be told, I have never flown in my life. Planes scare the mess out of me, and I don't scare easily. You ever been on a plane? I know most white people love them. My son-in-law tried his best to get me on a plane. I think he was pushing so hard because if that plane dropped out the sky, he thinks he will get my money, but I got news for him, I put it in my will that my money will go to my grandchildren.

"Maybe that's why my husband did what he did. Cheated on me. Maybe he felt I wasn't willing to take risks."

"He cheated because that's what he wanted to do."

"Well said for such a young person! How old are you anyway?"

"Twenty-three."

"Twenty-three, that's a good age. It's the perfect age to go and discover the world, only do it with a suitcase, so you have more than just the clothes on your back."

She smiled at me, but I tried hard to fight back the tears.

"There I go again. I'm sorry. I have a knack for noticing things. I saw you come into the bus station and I noticed that you didn't have anything in your hands. What did they throw you out for? Drugs? Pregnant? Black boyfriend?"

I couldn't hold back the tears anymore.

She reached into her purse and pulled out a Kleenex. "There, there. I knew you needed to cry the moment I looked into your eyes. Pain recognizes pain. You cry all you want. Shoot, I started crying the moment I found out about my husband was cheating on me. Then, I cried even harder because he was killed and then the tears just fell because it was obvious he just didn't love me anymore. I think I cried the most because of that.

"We're women. It's what we do to push through the moments in life that touch us with unkindness. We cry."

NINETEEN

"It was my stepmother, she threw me out because she said I was a..."

"Go ahead girl, speak through your pain. You aren't going to say anything to me that will shock me."

I could barely get the word to slip down to the tip of my tongue. "She said I was a Negro."

"Well, I guess I lied. That did shock me."

She touched my cheek. "My mother use to tell me that people who hate people because of their skin color, hate themselves. That's why I don't hate white people, I dislike some of them, but never hate. I love myself too much for that foolishness."

"What's it like?"

"What's, what like?"

"Being a black woman?"

"Girl, this bus trip isn't long enough to answer that question. You just go through life being you. Let other's fret over your skin color or lack of it that is. I think your real problem is that you're afraid to tell people that you're black. You're scared of how they will treat you. How they will look at you. Like I said before, be you. Let people draw their own conclusions.

"For the time being, try to think of yourself not as black or white, but as a woman. A beautiful young woman. Promise me that Lorraine, promise me that you will learn what it means to be a woman." She touched my chin.

"I promise."

"Good, because just being a woman will bring its own tribulations." She pulled out a sandwich, broke it in half and handed one of the halves to me. "Don't worry, we aren't about to have the Lord's Evening meal or something on this bus."

I laughed.

"Oh, my goodness, you laughed. It only took five hours or so, to get a laugh out of you. I thought this moment would never come." She laughed even more as she then pulled out a large bag of cheddar and caramel mixed popcorn. She poured some of the popcorn in a napkin and handed it to me. "I must like you...I don't share my popcorn with anybody. In fact, I must really like you to share this particular kind of popcorn with you. I had to have my driver go clear across town to get it for me."

"You really have a driver?"

"I do. You really black?"

I smiled. "I am."

"Glad we cleared that up. Now eat your sandwich and savor that popcorn. I ain't sharing the rest."

"Thank you," I whispered.

"You're welcome," she whispered back.

The outside world slowly drifted into the distance as we talked, ate, laughed and even a few times, cried. Dena cussed a few times as she spoke about her husband. She talked about how they met, what it was like falling in love for the first time and even what her first kiss felt like. I told her about Ella, daddy and ole big bones.

When the driver announced that we were pulling in for a two-hour rest break and a driver change, just outside Lexington Kentucky, I felt like I had known her my whole life.

"Come on. I think there's a clothing store not too far from the station that's in walking distance. Let's go get you some clothes and a suitcase, my treat." She looked at the boy who had been staring at me and raised her voice just loud enough for him to hear, as we walked by to exit the bus. "Having a little baggage in your life keeps the boys away. Don't you agree, Lorraine?"

I laughed. "Yes, ma'am, I guess it does."

For a moment, I felt a spark of happiness, a twinge of freedom and the touch of hope. For a moment, I felt like maybe I was going to be okay. But just as my feet touched the pavement, a young girl walked by who reminded me of Ella and my heart went back to that place, that place where my whole world was centered around protecting her.

Dena saw me staring at the girl. She grabbed my hand. "She will be okay. She will understand why you left. It will take some time, but that day will come."

"I was all she had," I said, through my tears.

"No you weren't, and frankly, I blame your father for making you feel like that was the case. It's his time now. It's his time to be a father. It's not your responsibility to raise your sister. Shoot, it wasn't your responsibility to raise yourself. It was his." She pulled me around and stood me in front of her. "You know what I see when I look at you? I see a young woman who hasn't allowed the strength and courage within her to reach its full potential. Strength, courage, love. Those are the backbones of any woman. Black or white. They breathe in us. Allow yourself to feel them. Let them carry you on this journey. Don't be afraid of them and don't let guilt suck you back into a world of hurt.

"Moving forward doesn't mean you lose the people in your past that mean the most to you. It means that you will not be standing in the same place, you were yesterday. The ones that matter, they will be at your finish line. Not on the sidelines. The finish line, that's where you will find your Ella, I promise."

She wiped away my tears. "Can we go shopping now?"

I hugged her. "Yes, we can go shopping now."

"Good, because I firmly believe that shopping takes away all sorts of injurious and painful things."

TWENTY

We made it back from the clothing store, within minutes of the bus getting ready to pull off. The bus driver gave us a nasty look as Dena handed him my suitcase.

"What are you going to do for money once you get to Atlanta?" She asked after we were settled back in our seats.

"I don't know. To be honest, I didn't get a chance to give it much thought. Everything happened so fast."

"What skills do you have?"

"I know how to cook and clean. I thought maybe I could get a job as a waitress or something until I find..."

"Until you find your birth mother? I was wondering about that. Didn't you tell me that your father said that she came to Chicago to go to College? How do you know that she isn't still in Chicago?"

"I don't. I guess I just figured that if she were, she would have..."

"Tried to contact you?"

I glanced down at my hands. "Yes."

Dena placed her hand on mine. "Lorraine, I know this is going to hurt what I'm about to say, and I don't in any way mean it to but...why would she go back to the place that she ran away from, especially given the reason?"

I thought about her question for a moment. "I guess... I suppose I just needed a direction. When I stood at the bus station's ticket window, and the lady asked me where I was headed, it was the only place that came to my mind."

"I see."

"I don't know who I really am. I need to find her. I need to look in her eyes. I need to see her..."

"Face. You want to see if you look like her. If she's as white as you or as black as me."

"Maybe."

"Not maybe. Maybe, is something one says when they're unsure about something. Deep down, you know why you want to find your birth mother. You need confirmation. You also want to tell her how your life turned out. You want her to know how much you suffered at the hands of Clarisse, or Ole big bones, as you called her. Am I right?"

I didn't respond.

"Lorraine, am I right?"

"Yes."

"Then know that you would be giving up something vital."

"What's that?"

"Your memories. For thirteen years, you had the touch of a beautiful mother. You have a sister who loves you. Consider this, if things had of been different, there would be no Ella. Those memories are real, Lorraine. They are breathing inside you. Who knows if your life with your birth mother wouldn't have turned out to be just as painful as Clarisse made it. Then there's the other thing..."

"What other thing?"

She took my hand into hers. "Think about what that man did to her. She has to live with that for the rest of her life. I'm sure she thought what she did was the best thing for you."

"No, I don't believe that. I believe it was the best thing for her. You don't understand, how could you!"

"Lower your voice. I'm your friend, but don't get it twisted, I'm a fifty-year-old grown woman, and you are a twenty-three-year-old young woman acting like a ten-year-old child. I'm just trying to help you, Lorraine."

"I didn't ask for your help."

"No, you didn't, but you needed it, so I'm going to let you have this moment. When you are ready to speak to me like you have returned to your real age, let me know."

I knew she was right, but I needed someone to blame. Someone to take the fall for my tears. Someone to place the weight of my sorrows upon.

We both sat in silence for a few minutes.

. "You think I don't understand Lorraine, but I do. I grew up in a foster home. I never knew my mother. Never had a father, not even a drunk one. These earrings that I have on, I purchased them just before I was married. I had them mailed to myself so I could pretend they were from my mother. The one I never knew. I know how it feels to want to face the woman that gave you up just so you could tell her how your life turned out. I know what it's like to want to see them hurt the way you've hurt. I'm not a stranger to that game."

I saw the tears in Dena's eyes.

"I also know what it's like to be raped. To have your dignity taken away from you. The woman at the foster care home that I grew up in always had different men dropping by. Most of them just acted as if I didn't exist. But there was one that if I could, I would have gone to prison for and that's real talk. He didn't just take away my dignity, he almost took away my will to keep living. Several times I tried. Several times I tried to end it all, but each time, my heart won. It fought to stay beating. It's like it knew. It knew there was hope in my bones.

"I went to a run-down public high school, but there was this one home economics teacher who saw something in me. She took me under her wing. Adopted me in every sense and helped me to feel the strength that I had. She encouraged me and wiped away the tears until the day came when they no longer fell or was felt on my skin.

"She taught me to sew, and I discovered that I had a knack for it. I could sew the mess out anything, even without a pattern. I started designing and sewing my own clothes, and soon other girls were paying me to design and sew their dresses. That's how I paid my way through college. After college, I opened a boutique clothing store that sold one-of-a-kind gowns. Today, I own three boutique clothing stores. Two in Chicago and one in New York.

"Lorraine, over the years I made many mistakes, and I blamed them all on her. The mother that gave me up the day I was born. I blamed her, for me loving money more than my own daughter at times. I blamed her, for me not understanding what love was or how to express it. In fact, if it was bad and it happened to me, she was my reason."

"Did you ever look for her?"

"I did. I'm not going to lie. I sunk thousands of dollars into private investigator after private investigator until one day I realized that I was blaming her for everything when I never knew her reason for doing what she did."

"So, you're saying that my birth mother's reason for giving me up was right?"

"We'd like to think that there could be no possible reason for a mother to give up her child, but life teaches you that, that's not always the case. I'm not saying it's right and I'm not saying it's wrong. I'm just saying that in the game of life, there are always exceptions to the rules. I can't pretend that I can walk in your birth mother's shoes, but I can say that I understand what size she might have worn."

She squeezed my hand.

"Now, you said you can cook and clean, don't' worry I'm not going to ask you to come and be my maid or something." She winked at me. "Do you know anything about computers?"

"I got very good grades in computers in high school."

"How good?"

"Pretty good I guess. I got a scholarship to go to College for Computer Engineering, but I didn't want to leave Ella. I had applied for the local technical college that wasn't too far from the house, but we didn't have the money for me to attend that one."

"I see. Did you really want to go to college for computers?"

"Kind of, it was the only way for me to..."

"Escape, but you didn't want to leave Ella."

"Right."

"Have you ever actually thought about what you really wanted to do in life, Lorraine? I mean, every girl dreams of something. Be it wedding dresses or white picket fences, there is something that drives her passion for growing up. What was yours?"

I stared out the window.

"There is something, isn't it?"

I nodded.

"Well, don't leave an older, but super-fine woman hanging. Tell me what it is."

"It's..."

"It's what?"

"I like to sing."

Dena turned her whole body toward me. "Can you?"

"I use to sing to Ella when she was little."

"Sweetie, singing to your little sister is not the same as singing out there in the real world. It takes a lot of voice to make it in the music world and connections if I might add."

"You asked me what my passion is, it's always been that."

She leaned back in her seat again and stared at the ceiling of the bus. "But again, can you? I mean, there's a difference between singing and blowing. Which one can you do?" She looked over at me.

"My daddy said I could...blow."

"Really? He's a white man, so he doesn't count. Do you think you can blow?"

"I believe so."

"You never 'believe so' when it comes to your passion. That shows doubt in yourself. Doubt in your ability. Doubters are not dream makers. Doubters sit on the bench waving their doubter flag as the dream makers run pass them.

"My foster mother was a doubter. She would wave her doubter flag every time I turned on my sewing machine. Doubters should never see the front of you. Only the back. You understand me?"

"Yes, I do."

"Good, now let's hear what you got."

"What, now?"

"Yes, now."

I looked around and felt as if every pair of eyes were staring at me.

Mrs. D, knew I was stalling. "The people on this bus will either love it or hate it, but, at least you'll know for sure if you've got something or not. Now open them lungs girl, and make this bus jump."

"Seriously?"

"Seriously, you're the one that said it was your passion. You should never be afraid to put your passion out in the air. Passion is what makes the world of success, smell good. Go ahead, do your thing. I'm listening."

I cleared my throat, closed my eyes and placed my hand over the key that sat in my front pocket. If I couldn't use it to open my locket, I could use it to open my voice.

The applause made the bus shake. Even the bus driver was clapping. The boy who had been staring at me earlier stood up and started his way toward us.

"Boy, go back to your seat. She doesn't have time for you."

I laughed through my tears, and when that moment of happiness hit me again, I still thought of Ella, but I knew, I knew this is what she would have wanted for me too.

TWENTY-ONE

"I want you to go to New York."

"New York?"

"Yes, New York. See, I never mentioned my daughter's name the whole time you and I spoke because of who she is. Remember how I said that I wanted her to get her husband to sign a Prenup?"

"I do."

"Well, it wasn't just my money that I was worried about, it's hers. My daughter's name is..."

She leaned over and whispered it in my ear.

When she sat back in her seat again, I thought I was going to scream. All I could do was silently mouthed the name of one of the biggest female R & B singers to come out of Chicago—Semeerah Fox.

"I'm surprised you knew who she was."

"Anyone who listens to the radio knows who she is. Even my father knows her. I still have every CD of hers that he brought me."

"Nice, I've to thank him for contributing to her career fund."

"Yeah, he had his moments," I said as I sighed.

"No sad talk! Let's talk about what I just suggested—New York."

"I can't go to New York."

"Look, I know how important it is for you to find your birth mother, so this what I'll do—I'll look for her for you. You said that she came to Chicago to attend college, so it can't be that hard."

"You would do that for me?"

"I'll have someone start right away. I promise."

She saw the hesitation on my face.

"Look, I have an apartment in New York that I only use when I have to visit the store. You could stay there. I need someone to work the computer more at that store than the one in Chicago, anyway. Our biggest orders come through that store, and I'm losing money because no one can figure out how to use the new software program that I had installed to handle our inventory system. This would work for the both of us. You said you were good with computers. You could work in the store during the day and hit the recording studio in the evening with my daughter, once she comes back through."

"How do you know your daughter will even consider me?"

"She's putting together her own record label, but no one knows about that. She doesn't want people to start talking, especially since she's so young, but she's been in the game now for ten years. It's a good move for her. She's been a little unfocused lately, but once she's back on her game, she'll be looking for talent. You've got talent."

I was speechless but still hesitant.

"I'll even pay for your ticket to New York. The bus will take another rest stop in Detroit. I'll purchase your ticket and send you on your way."

"Why? Why would you do all that for me?"

"You're not the first one I've helped. It's what I do. Someone did it for me, so, I make it my business to do it for others. It's not about me paying it forward, it's about me helping someone to move forward. We all got reasons that may have caused us to get stuck in life. Besides, there is someone else you should want to get back at?"

"Who?"

"Old Big Bones."

We both laughed.

"When I opened my second boutique store in Chicago, I took a picture of me standing in front of it, which I then had hand-delivered to my foster mother, along with a small white flag that had the word, 'doubter' and huge red X covering it.

"The day it was delivered, I pulled up in my white Mercedes and watched from across the street as the postman gave her the letter."

"You didn't."

"I did. Let me tell you, the look on her face when she realized it was me, that moment…that moment was priceless."

I reached in my front pocket and pulled out the key. I stared at it for a few moments before putting it back. "I'll go. I'll go to New York."

PART THREE

TWENTY-TWO
Honour Blue Baker

It was almost dinner time when I walked down the hallway towards my mother's hospital room. My tears were dry but still fresh in my mind.

I saw Bryan standing behind the nurse's station.

"Honour. What are you doing back here? I thought you were going to try and get some rest."

"Hi, Bryan. I was hoping that a cot could be brought into my mother's room. I can't leave her."

"Of course." He asked one of the nurses to take care of it for me, and we both watched as the nurse got someone on the phone that could bring the cot. When she placed the phone down, Bryan pulled me off to the side. "You want to go and grab something to eat in the cafeteria? I've got about an hour or so before I have to make my rounds again."

"Sure." He reached for my hand. I hesitated at first but extended mine. Neither of us said a word more until we were seated in the cafeteria.

"I wish we were seeing each other again under these circumstances, Honour. I wanted to call you so many times over the years, but..."

"Life got in the way."

"Something like that. So how long have you been seeing Aaron? Is it serious?"

"We started dating a year ago, but I've known him for a few years. He's my tax attorney. He owns a pretty good-sized firm in Chicago."

"Is it serious?"

"He asked me to marry him yesterday."

"Of course you said no."

"How do you know that?"

"Because he cheated on you. I could see it in your eyes when you looked at him, and when you two spoke to each other, you could tell there was a lot of pain there."

"It's a long story."

"No, it's not. When my ex-wife went outside our marriage, it wasn't a long story. It was just a 'done' one."

"It's not that easy."

"It's never easy when you love someone."

I placed the fork on my plate and looked out the window we were sitting in front of. "Did you consider forgiving her? Could you?"

"Don't ask me that."

"Why not?"

"Because what you really want to know is, if I would have stayed married to her."

"That's obvious. Here you are."

"I did. I stayed. I tried to forgive and forget as the good book tells us to do. Like my mother taught me. I didn't want to give up on our marriage, but, a year later, we were right back there again."

I leaned back in my chair. "That's my fear."

"I'm not going to sit here and tell you Honour, that just because my wife did it again, he will. But, I will say this...only you can determine if you want to go into a marriage with fear lurking at the doorway. Every marriage will have problems. It will face trials and tribulations, but that should never be one of them."

"We don't live in a perfect world, Bryan."

"No, we don't. But we can love perfectly, even with an imperfect heart. We can be true to the person we vowed to spend the rest of our lives with. If it weren't possible, we would never have been told to do it."

"You sound like your mother."

"I know. It's scary sometimes, but I appreciate the morals she tried to instill in me."

"She did a good job."

We watched a few people come into the cafeteria. Neither of us, actually eating what was on our plates.

"So, did you go by there?"

"Go by where?" I asked.

"The King's house?"

I stared at him. I never told him. I never told anyone... except for Aaron.

"Why are you asking me that?"

"I know, Honour. I've always known. I can even tell you the day it happened."

I clenched my fist to keep the tears at bay. "How did you know?"

"That day, I saw you leaving their house. I saw the tears in your eyes. At first, I thought I was wrong, but when I saw your dress. I knew. I wanted to kill him for it. I thought about it. I really did."

"What!"

"It's true. I wanted to hurt him because he had hurt you. I confronted him."

"You didn't."

"I did."

"What, what did he say?"

"He laughed in my face. He said that he would never dare consider touching a...."

"He used that word, didn't he?"

"Yes. Yes, he did. I punched him and then I kept hitting him, until, I looked into his eyes and saw how pathetic he was. I made him confess to me that he did it. I made him say the words. The truth. I just wish I would have done it in front of someone who could have done something more about it."

My eyes. My eyes were filled with tears. They fell upon my plate. Mixed in with the juice of my green beans. "Why, why did you do it?"

"You know why. You've always known."

"Bryan, I don't know what to say..."

"You don't have to say anything. I just wanted you to know that someone out here knows what he did to you. Someone who really loves you. I've always really loved you."

He reached over and took my hand.

"I'm not going to make it difficult for you. I know you have a lot going on. But, I want you to know that now that we're here, I'm not backing away."

"Well, you need too!"

"Aaron, I didn't see you standing there. What are you doing here?"

"I went to check on you at the hotel after I got my room to see if you wanted to have dinner or something, but they said you never came back there, so I assumed you came back here."

He stared at Bryan's hand on top of mine.

"Can we talk, Honour?"

"I need to go anyway. I'll stop by your mother's room after my rounds, you're coming later, right?"

I nodded my head as Bryan leaned over, lifted up my hand and placed a kiss upon it.

"We'll both be there."

Bryan gave Aaron a smirk. "Bye, Honour."

I watched Bryan leave and Aaron took a seat.

"Just friends, huh?"

"Don't start."

"Don't do this, Honour. Revenge doesn't look good on you. I know I hurt you...but please don't do this."

"It's not about revenge Aaron, only you would think so."

"So what is it? You have feelings for him? You haven't seen him in years."

"I need to go."

"That's your answer? Walking away?"

"How am I walking away Aaron, I'm going to my mother's room and didn't you just say you were going there with me?"

He stood up. He tried to reach for my hand, but I wouldn't give it. It still had Bryan's touch on it, and I wasn't' sure what I wanted to do with that kind of intimacy just yet.

TWENTY-THREE

Aaron sat in the chair beside me as I switched on the television. I waited. I knew he wouldn't let the question he had asked me early, go to rest. I could see it still lingering in his thoughts. I admit, I enjoyed the moment. The agony that he was in, as he contemplated something he hadn't thought possible...someone else.

I knew it wasn't right for me to feel that way. To slowly digest a small piece of revenge pie, but the feeling was there, and I enjoyed the flavor.

"You didn't answer my question?"

"What question, Aaron?"

He leaned forward and tried to make eye contact with me. "Do you have feelings for him?"

"I've known Bryan a long time." I kept my eyes on the television.

"That's not an answer."

"It's the only one I can give you."

"Honour, look at me."

I kept glancing at the television although I couldn't tell you what was on.

He reached up and touched my cheek to get my attention. "Can you just look at me, please?"

I turned the television down, and our eyes met.

"I want to marry you Honour."

I stared at my mother to break the connection. "Let's not talk about that now Aaron. Besides, it's late, and I'm tired."

"Would you be tired if Bryan walked in here?"

I stood up. "Probably not," I said, as I walked over toward the window. It was mean and nasty, but, it was also the truth.

"Do you want me to beg? Because I will. I love you that much. I'll do whatever I need to."

I could see the street down below. I could see people walking by as if they didn't have a care in the world. I wished...I wished I could have joined them. "I'm not asking you to beg Aaron. I just need time."

He got up and came and stood behind me. His hands rested on my waist. His lips barely touching my neck as he spoke. "Before this evening, I think I could have given you that, but now that another person is playing for your heart, I can't. I won't."

I turned toward him. "This is not a game." His eyes sunk into mine and messed with my emotions. His hands reached around to the small of my back, and he drew me toward him.

"No, it's a war, and I intend to win Honour. I intend to make you my wife."

I could feel my legs trembling. My heart pounding. I struggled to say something...anything. "It's a shame you didn't have this determination before you cheated." I tried to gently push away, but, he wouldn't let go. There was not a drop of space between us.

"You're right. It is." Our lips brushed.

The door opened.

"Honour Blue Baker."

I moved quickly, freeing myself from Aaron's embrace. "Jimmy, I haven't seen you in ages."

I glanced at Aaron. He gave me a sly grin.

"That's because you don't come home often, and it's Sheriff Jimmy now."

I could feel my heart beginning to settle back down as I straighten out my blouse. "My mother told me that you picked up where your father left off."

"I'm sorry to hear about what's happy with your mama, Honour. I hope she pulls through."

We both glanced over at Mama.

"I do too. So, what can I do for you, Sheriff Jimmy?"

He laughed as I walked over and took a seat next to mama's bed.

"I wanted to let your mother know about that young girl she found in the river up at Thompson Bay Bridge. I meant to come see her before now, I kind of bombarded her with questions when the girl was first found. I think she thought I was treating her like a suspect. It's just we ain't never had a situation like that one before. I hope she isn't too mad."

"I'm sure she will forgive you. I heard about that girl. Mama thought she was dead."

"So did we, but they were able to save her. Weirdest thing I've ever seen. I think the whole town has been affected by that situation. Folks still talking about it. The papers even wanted to interview the girl, but we aren't allowing that right now. They might be interviewing me later, we'll see.

"We're still conducting our investigation. Although, since she ain't dead, it doesn't leave us much of a case to investigate."

Jimmy seemed too disappointed about that fact. "How is the girl doing?"

"She's doing okay. The doctors say it will take some time, but that she will make a full recovery. Seems she slipped on the rocks as she was trying to cross over the river. People don't realize how deep that river is."

"I remember Bryan and I playing in that river when I was a little girl."

"Kids still play in it today. Times I guess, don't change that much. I heard Bryan was back as well. Haven't seen him yet."

I caught Aaron staring at me.

"I saw him just a bit earlier. Still the same Bryan, just a doctor now."

"That's not what the nurses been saying. I heard them talking about him as I walked by. I don't think there is one nurse that doesn't have a crush on him. He always was a super smart guy. Guess he wasn't smart enough to catch you through. You know everyone thought the two of you would have..."

"Sheriff Jimmy." Aaron walked over and extended his hand. "I'm Aaron. Honour's fiancé."

Jimmy laughed as he shook Aaron's hand. "Well, I guess that explains why Honour was in your arms when I walked in the room. Forgive me. I didn't mean anything by it. My congrats to you both." He glanced over at me. "I guess that's a shame for old Bryan, huh?"

"So," I stated, "were you able to get in touch with the girl's family? Mama said she was young."

"She ain't talking much. We've inquired a few times, but the girl won't tell us. She just keeps stating that she's looking for the Kings."

"Did she say why?"

"Nope, we think she's related to them somehow."

"Did you ask her if she was related?"

Jimmy looked at me. Obviously, he had not.

"We're taking it slow. Once we know she's more on the mend, we'll go in deeper with the questions."

"I see. I'm sure that's smart."

"That's what I told the guys. Anyway, I just stopped by to look in on your mother and to say hi to you. I only heard you were in town a couple of days ago. How's that fancy hair salon of yours going? Anyone famous been in it that I know? I hear you get celebrities all the time."

I glanced at Aaron. "You know I can't tell you my client's business. Anyway, I'm in the process of making some changes with it."

He winked at me. "Gotcha. I thought about moving to Chicago. Even considered New York or South Carolina. Changes are good. Congrats again; hope I will get an invitation to the wedding."

Aaron spoke up before I could respond.

"We'll make sure your name is on the list. Wouldn't want to leave out any of the guys Honour grew up with."

Jimmy laughed. "Good one."

I watched as Jimmy left the room. My eyes never leaving Aaron. As soon as I heard the door close, I lit into him.

"You are not my fiancé, Aaron. I never agreed to marry you."

"I know that."

He stepped toward me. "I can see it in your eyes you know."

I immediately looked toward the floor. "What, what is it you think you see?"

"How much you love me."

He grabbed me by the waist and tried to pull me close. "We can pick up where we left off."

"Aaron don't."

"I love you Honour."

Once again it took all I had to pull away. "This is not going to work."

"Sure it is." He pulled me back, wrapping his arms around me and whispering in my ear.

"Say you'll marry me, Honour Blue Baker."

I could feel him breathing on my neck. "Aaron..."

"Say you'll become my wife." He placed his lips on my neck. "Say you'll be mine."

I saw them. The picture was so vivid. I could see him with her just as clear as I could the day I opened my office door. I could see that smirk upon her face that I wanted to smack clear off. The tears came. They slipped down my cheeks with ease. It was never going to go away.

"I can't."

"Please, Honour. I promise; I'm a good man. I'll love you. I'll never hurt you again. You can trust me, baby. I swear you can trust me."

Trust. That word stuck in my head like a force to be dealt with. It was like the period of a sentence. It was in the end, the only thing that mattered.

I pulled away slowly and allowed an arm's length of distance to come between us. "I'm sorry Aaron, I can't."

"What are you saying Honour?"

"I'm saying that I can't marry you. You're right, I love you, Aaron. I really do. But I have to be able to trust you. When I was a little girl, my mama always taught me that while love is the foundation, it's trusting that holds the walls of any relationship up. I never understood what she really meant by those words until now. "

"Can you trust Bryan?"

I wanted to slap him.

"Bryan is not in this conversation, you and I are." I came at him, fast and furious. "Bryan is not the one who cheated on me. You are. Bryan is not the one who hurt me. You did that. Remember?"

He took a few steps back. "You're right. I'm sorry. Look maybe I am pushing you too much. I'm just scared of losing the best thing that has ever happened to me. "

I tried to soften my voice. "Aaron, I don't think I'm going to change my mind."

"No, I'm not hearing that right now. I'm not accepting it."

I walked back over to my chair and opened my purse. I took out the velvet box and held it toward him. "Take it, Aaron."

"I'm not taking that Honour."

"Please."

"I'm not taking it. I mean that Honour. I'll go back to Chicago, I'll give you some space, but this isn't over between us."

"Aaron."

"Look, I'll give you a week."

I looked at him.

"Okay, two weeks. But, if I don't hear from you Honour, I'm coming back here. I'll move here if I have to."

"You wouldn't."

"Yes, I would."

He took a few steps toward me, placed a kiss on my cheek and wrapped my hands around the velvet box.

"That belongs to you. I hope your mother will be okay, I really do because I want her to see how much I love you."

I watched him saunter towards the door. I'm not going to lie; my heart was trying to take over. I could see it urging me to stop him. It kept making me feel as if I were making the biggest mistake of my life. I could see it looking for the eraser. I could see it trying to blot out the picture of him with her, and replacing it with future pictures of us, in my head. Happy pictures.

If only they were real. If only they were true. Were they the possibility or the fantasy?

"Aaron." He stopped, and when he turned toward me, I could see the tears in his eyes.

I stood there with my heart in my hand. Afraid to hand it to him. "How do I know? How do I know that you won't do it again?"

Before he could answer, a loud noise echoed into the air. It shook the walls and demanded my attention. I realized that it was coming from my mother. From her heart machine. I began to scream. Nurses flew into the room within seconds. I was once again ushered out into the hallway just as I saw Bryan running down the corridor.

Our eyes met as he disappeared into my mother's room and the door closed.

TWENTY-FOUR

Once again, I was a door watcher.

Parts of me begging it to open. Parts of me scared of what I might hear, once it did open, and every part of me wanting to run through it and beg my mama to wake up.

As I sat, Aaron held my hand. He rubbed my back. He wiped away my tears, but the only man at that time that could ease my pain was in that room.

Bryan.

Mama always thought I never paid him any attention. But she was wrong. I always knew. I always knew how he felt. That day, the day I went to the King's home, I had finally mustered up the courage to tell him that I felt the same, that I was in love with him.

Finally, the door opened, and Bryan and a nurse stepped out. I jumped to my feet. I scanned her face. The nurse smiled as she turned to walk down the hallway.

Bryan placed his hands on my shoulders and looked me in the eyes. "She's still in a coma. She had another stroke that took away the use of her left side. We're not sure if the loss is permanent yet. We're going to run some tests, but it's going to be difficult to determine the depth of the damage until she wakes up. It's her heart, however, that we're more concerned with. We're bringing in a Specialist."

I placed my hand over my mouth to keep from screaming.

"Do you think she will wake up?" Aaron asked.

"We certainly hope so. I do know that woman in there, that woman is a fighter. Where do you think her daughter gets it from?"

We heard his name being paged over the intercom.

"I need to go and sign a release for another patient. I'll be back as soon as I can. I've had your mother's doctor paged. He was in surgery, but he'll be here at soon as possible." He placed a kiss on my cheek. Out the corner of my eye, I could see Aaron's face. I knew he wanted to say something, but he held back.

Aaron pulled out his cell phone.

"What are you doing?"

"Leaving a message for my assistant. I'm going to have her route any of my calls to my cell and cancel all of my appointments for this week."

"Aaron, maybe you should..."

"I'm staying, Honour. I'll have her send my files to the hotel, and I'll work from there this week. I'll give you some space Honour, but there is no way I'm leaving."

He grabbed my hand. "I'm going to head to the hotel. I really think you should come as well and try to sleep there tonight. You know you aren't going to get any rest on that cot."

I shook my head no.

"What's your room number?"

"4B, why?"

"I'm going to have them move my room next to yours." He placed a soft kiss on my lips. "I love you. I'll bring you a change of clothes in the morning. I'll be here for breakfast."

TWENTY-FIVE

I was sitting by my mother's bed with the lights dimmed when Bryan walked in. I felt his hand on my shoulder.

"The sun is going to be up in a few hours. You should try to get some sleep."

I looked toward the poor little cot on the other side of my mother's bed. "You've probably been here longer than I have."

"I'm a doctor, that's what doctors do."

"Well, I'm a daughter. That's what daughters do."

We both chuckled softly as he pulled a chair up next to mine.

"Her doctor is still tied up, but he is aware of the situation."

"Thank you. You look tired."

"I am, but at least I'm off duty now."

"It's almost two in the morning Bryan, you should go home."

"I will, but I wanted to stop in and see you before I did."

"I keep thinking that any moment now she will wake up and start complaining about her wig not being on correctly."

He placed his hand on top of mine. I glanced down at it.

"I meant what I said, your mother is a fighter."

"I know." I pulled my hand away.

"When you looked at me just a second ago, I could see the moon in your eyes."

I looked down. "So, tell me, besides becoming a doctor and getting divorced, what else have you been up to for the last twenty-three years or so?"

He leaned back slightly in his chair. Our eyes connected for a second and a small smile slid across his face.

He always had such a kind smile.

"Well, I wrote and had a book published. Traveled some. That's how I met Stephanie. My ex-wife. I was in London. She was there for a book event that one of the authors she represented was having. She's a literary agent for a major book publisher in New York."

"How convenient for you."

"I know right."

"How long were you two married?"

"Five years. I found out about the first affair, about one year and a half into our marriage. It was with one of her authors' of course."

"You still sound bitter."

"In some ways, I guess. I just wish I had taken the warning signs seriously."

"What warning signs?"

Bryan looked at me. "Honour, let's not do this. Let's not compare notes on our pain."

"You're right. Let's talk about something else."

"I thought about you. I thought about you all the time. To be honest, the moment I proposed to my ex-wife, I thought of you. I'm ashamed to admit that but it's true."

"Bryan."

"I know we haven't seen each other in a long time, and perhaps we're different people now or maybe we're the same, with just grown up ways of looking at life. I don't know. But, I want to find out.

"After graduation from high school, you talk about how life was like a staircase and how every day we can choose to take one step into the possibilities that it has for us. I've never forgotten that. It's why I became a doctor. Every day, I am given a moment to save a life. I take that moment and look for every possibility I can find to help that person."

He reached for my hand, and I allowed him to take it this time. "I know this is bad timing, in more ways than one, but, I can't let this moment leave us without stepping completely into it and trying out all the possibilities I know are there."

"Bryan, I wish things were different. I wish we could have met again before Aaron and I started dating, but it didn't happen that way."

"Honour, I know that you never had any feelings for me, not in that way. Not in the way that I wanted. Did you know that after high school, I wanted to ask you to marry me? I know it was a crazy idea. We were young, too young some may have thought, but I wanted to marry you. Sometimes I wonder if that's why Stephanie and I really didn't work. Sometimes I think she knew. She knew that my heart never truly belonged to her. "

"It wasn't a crazy idea."

Even in the moonlight, our eyes could find each other at just the right time.

"Don't play with me Honour. Don't tell me something like that unless you really mean it."

"I did. Back then."

He leaned back in his chair. "My mother said it, but I didn't think it was possible. She told me to wait until after college and then if I felt the same way to go after you. Only after college, I went to Medical school."

"Then you met Stephanie."

"Then I met Stephanie."

Silence knocked on the door, and we let it in for awhile.

"I've never wanted to turn back the clock of time as much I want to now." He took my hand again. "I have to know Honour. I have to hear you say it. Even if you don't mean it now, for my own selfish sanity, I need to hear the words fall from your lips...did you love me?"

"Yes, Bryan. Yes, I loved you." I could feel his body moving closer to mine. I could feel the next moment.

The moment when he kissed me.

"Bryan," I whispered, as I eased away, "we can't live in the past."

"I'm not asking you too. When I kissed you just now, it was for the future. It was a promise of my heart. I wanted you to feel what it's like to have a man kiss you that you will never have to doubt. You will never have to wonder if he'll be true to you. One that will always cherish you as a man should cherish a woman. You deserve that Honour. You deserve me."

"This is not fair to Aaron. He's trying so hard to make up for it. He loves me, Bryan. He really does."

"I know that. I know that he loves you, but your heart is like a puzzle, and I am the only one that will ever fit it, perfectly. Tell me I'm wrong."

I didn't respond.

He stood up and walked toward the door. "That kiss just proved one thing."

"What's that?"

"True love, real love, endures all things, even time."

TWENTY-SIX
Lorraine

Fear ripped through my body as the bus driver made the announcement. We had finally arrived in Michigan. I looked at Mrs. D as she paid for my bus ticket to New York, she was so sure, so confident. I felt like a little child hiding behind her fur coat. She squeezed my hand. "What if I get to New York and…"

"No doubts. Only belief. I can't be the only one who believes in you. You've got to believe in yourself. You've spent twenty-three years looking after your little sister, that you forget to think about you. Your dreams. Now, I can't promise a singing career, I can only try to create the opportunity, but if you don't believe in yourself, then the opportunity will be nothing but that. You understand?"

I grabbed her and hugged her again. "I'm going to miss you."

She began to laugh. "I wish my own daughter would hug me like that. That child can't stand me most times. Shoot, I can't stand her most times. But that's how it goes between mothers and daughters. Now, I've made arrangements for Kevin, my store manager to pick you up at the bus station once you arrive. He'll be in our company car. It has the store's logo and my name on it. He's been running my New York store for ten years. Started working for me right after high school. He's sharp as a whip and bossy as all get out, but you'll love him. Most of the staff there is around your age. I like young folks working for me because they work harder and want success more.

You'll soon fit right in if you heed the advice I gave you earlier about believing in yourself.

"Now, Kevin will also give you a key to my apartment. It's nothing fancy, but you can make it home, just don't touch anything."

I laughed, but I knew she was probably serious.

"You can take the room next to the guest bathroom. Melinda is my housekeeper when I'm in town. She'll be there to help you get settled in. She's an old, feisty Southern woman, but she can also cook her tail off, best believe. I forgot to tell you that I left a message for my daughter. Hopefully, she will get it and come by and see you. She's preparing for a tour so it may take a minute. "

She saw the worried look on my face.

"Don't worry, I'll get the two of you together. My daughter knows I have a knack for three things, sewing, business and discovering talent. I use to say four, but obviously, marriage is no longer my thing."

I saw the sadness in her eyes as she stared off for a moment.

"I'll try to get to New York after the funeral if I can. You'll be in good hands with Kevin."

She reached into her coat pocket and pulled out some money.

"I have money."

She laughed. "Child, you are going to New York, not Atlanta. You'll need this, trust me."

The bus driver announced that the bus to Atlanta was leaving.

"I'll be okay, really."

"Okay." She placed the money back into her pocket. "Call me if you need anything, day or night. Kevin will get you set up on the payroll, and he knows how to reach me."

As she turned quickly toward the bus, a young man that had been standing behind her, accidently bumped into her. He apologized, but I could tell Mrs. D, wasn't happy about it. She gave him a stern look and rushed to get on the bus.

The bus driver made the announcement again indicating that it was the final call.

"Don't forget what I said Lorraine, believe in yourself, and pray I don't meet my husband's girlfriend and end up in jail! Tell Kevin to keep his phone on, just in case."

We both laughed as the bus doors closed, but I knew she was dead serious.

TWENTY-SEVEN

I saw him walking toward me. Backpack slung over his shoulder. Deep wavy hair, welcoming brown eyes and olive skin. You could see his dimples when he smiled. I put him in his early twenties, once I got a better look at his face. He had on a pair of jeans that had a few rips in them, a baseball cap, and a white t-shirt. Twenty-four, maybe.

"Do you mind if I sit here?"

I slid over to the window seat, and he threw his backpack on the seat between us.

"Is this your first time traveling to New York?"

"It is, why?"

"Just making conversation, that's all. It's a long trip. Thought I'd be friendly, plus, you don't look like a New Yorker."

I was tired and already missing Mrs. D. I leaned my head against the window as the bus began to pull out of the station.

"I have a few shirts in my backpack if you want something to lean your head on."

"I'm good." I could tell he was fishing for something else to say.

"My name is David."

"I'm Lorraine."

"Where you from? "

"Maywood."

"Cool. I got a friend who use to live in Maywood. He went to Proviso East High School. He graduated from there about five years back. You know it?"

"I do.".

"You don't talk much, I see." He reached into his backpack and pulled out a candy bar. "You want half?"

"I'm good, but thanks."

"You have any family in New York?"

I tried not to show my frustration at his constant barrage of questions.

"It's cool, you don't have to answer."

Five minutes passed.

"I'm headed to New York to get into the music industry. I'm new to it, to be honest, but I know I will make it. I've got just the right amount of determination and drive. You need those things to make it New York. It can be a tough place for someone new to it."

Since it was evident that he wasn't going to let me sleep, I sat up in my seat and tried to listen as he rambled on.

"You know they don't call New York the city of dreams for nothing. Anyone looking to get into the music industry goes to New York. It's the place to make dreams either live or die. Of course, many music wannabes get taken for a ride. Taken advantage of, you know what I mean?"

I shrugged my shoulders.

"It's true. See, people promise a lot of things. You'll meet a lot of those types of individuals in New York. I call them the dream killers. They pump you up with promises but can't deliver. I plan on delivering. New York is about who you know. You can't get anywhere in New York without knowing the right people. It's all about connections." He slaps one hand on top of the other. "You got to have connections, without them, you're dead. You know what I mean?"

"Not really," I casually said.

"You also got to have a talent. Real talent. It's got to be unique. I saw this black guy on television a few weeks back, tap dancing his butt off."

I laughed. "Tap dancing?"

"Yeah, laugh all you want, he had talent. Real talent. I bet he's got a great manager. It was a top notch movie."

"I was laughing at the way you describe the tap dancer.'"

"Well, he was black. I'm black. My mother is black."

I stop laughing. "Really, you're black?"

"Yeah, really."

"You don't look black."

"Now I should be the one offended."

"I'm sorry, I didn't mean anything by it, but you look...."

"Spanish."

"Yeah."

"I get that a lot."

"What about your father, he couldn't have been black?"

"That's funny, but you're right. My father wasn't. He was Spanish. He died when I was just a baby, so I have only seen pictures of him."

"How come you don't say that you're Spanish?"

"I don't make the rules."

"What rules?"

"The one-drop rule."

"The what?"

"You're kidding, right? You've never heard of the one-drop rule?"

"I haven't."

"I can't believe that. Your people made it up."

"What do you mean...my people?"

"You know...White folks."

"How do you know that?"

"Everybody knows that."

"So, what's the one-drop rule? Tell me."

"Man, I can't believe you don't know nothing about that. But okay, I'll take you to school. You look like you just graduated anyway." I gave him a nasty look. He smiled. "Just kidding. Anyway, the one drop rule is the foundation of racial classification. Back in the slavery days, it's how they determined if you were African or not. If they could prove you had at least one drop of black blood, they considered you to be a Negro. At first, it was a social law, some say it was a ploy to keep the white race pure. In fact, Tennessee made it law in 1910 and Virginia followed with that foolishness in 1924.

"My mother always told me that no one is 'pure' anything. We all got something running through our veins, and that's why everyone should just be classified as humans. You know, if you were half black and half white, you were considered Mulatto.

"It's true. In fact, Thomas Jefferson was said to have gotten with one. A mulatto. She was a slave, and her name was Sally Hemings. History says she was the illegitimate daughter of Jefferson's father in law and that she was three-fourth white. I've always wondered how they came up with that number, but, like I said, I didn't make the rules.

"Anyway, I read somewhere that after Jefferson and Heming's 'mulattoes' were considered free slaves, they were able to pass themselves as white people with no problem. Interesting huh?"

"Why are you looking at me like that?" I asked.

"Because, you should see your face."

"I'm just..."

"Shocked? I can tell. I personally don't care what you are, on the surface or underneath. See, to me, it's not about any of that. I've learned one thing in my twenty-four years of walking above ground... it's about your character. It's about what your bones are made out of."

"Really?"

"Yeah, really. I stole that last part from my mother, but I added my own flair to it."

I laughed. "So, it's just you and your mother?"

"Nah, she remarried this white dude about three years back. I also have a kid brother."

"You don't sound like you like him."

"I love my little brother. I'll do anything for him, best believe."

"No, I mean your stepfather."

"That fool. I hate him if you just want to know the truth about it."

"Why?"

"He's a low-down son-of-a-gun, that's why, but my mother acts like that doesn't matter because he has money. He also has a serious drinking problem. He would beat the crap out of my kid brother and me as often as he could. It's why I left. I knew my mother would never leave him. She likes his money too much."

"If your stepfather is so bad, why did you leave your younger brother there with him?"

"I had too. I can't take care of both of us. I only wish I would have gotten a chance to explain things to him. You know, help him to understand that I still got love for him."

He grew quiet.

"We don't have to talk about this anymore if you don't want to."

"You're right, maybe we shouldn't."

I didn't know what else to say, so I leaned my head against the window again and closed my eyes. A few hours later, I felt him tap me on the shoulder.

"Lorraine, you awake? I want to tell you the rest."

I opened my eyes slowly. "You don't have to."

"I know, but I want to."

I wiped my eyes and sat up in my seat.

"Two days ago, he came home real drunk. I mean drunker than I've ever seen him. He started in on me and before I knew it, he was hitting me so hard, I thought I was going to pass out. I felt like every drop of life was being beaten out of me."

"How did you get him to stop?"

"My mother finally remembered?"

"Remembered what?"

"That she was a mother."

"Wow."

"Wow, is right. If my mother hadn't stepped in and saved my butt, I might be dead right now. It was her that urged me to leave."

"Where was your little brother doing all of this?"

"He was upstairs. I always made him hide in our bedroom when that fool came home drunk. I'm scared for him, though."

"You think your stepfather will do something to your little brother?"

"He might. I did something stupid as I left the house."

"What did you do?"

"I saw his wallet on the table and..."

"You stole some of his money!"

"Don't let everybody on the bus know."

"I'm sorry."

"It's cool. My mother saw me take it, but she promised not to say anything. I can only hope that she keeps her word. For my brother's sake at least. If I could have done one thing differently, I would have said good-bye to him."

"I'm sure he will understand."

"I hope so. I really do. I feel like it was my responsibility to protect him. I guess that's why I'm so determined. I need to make something of myself, not just for me, but for the both of us. Every decision I make is for him. Every decision I make is so I can bring him to me. I have to get him out of that house. I promise you, that is going to happen."

He had me thinking about Ella and how I never got a chance to say good-bye. "What's your little brother's name?"

"Jeffery. He's twelve-years-old and a really good kid. He depended on me for everything, though. You know what I mean?"

"I do."

He smiled. "So you get it. That's cool."

"You have any connections in New York?" I asked, trying to change the subject.

He lowered his head. "I don't, but, I'm not going to let that deter me. I know it will be hard, but like I said, I'm determined. All I need is a chance. An opportunity. Once my feet hit the New York pavement, it's on. That's all I'm saying."

"I'm sure you will do great."

He nodded in agreement. "You never did tell me what's taking you to the Big Apple."

"I have a friend of mine who owns a clothing boutique. I'm pretty good with computers, so, she's giving me a job and a place to stay."

"That's what I call a hookup, but, you don't look like the computer type."

"What 'type' do I look like?"

"I don't know, but I can tell you, computers isn't it. You got to have something else hidden under that pretty face."

"Something like what?" I ignored the 'pretty face' part.

"You tap dance?"

We both laughed, but then it was my turn to go silent.

"I was right, wasn't I? You got some other mad skill, don't you?"

I nodded my head.

"Fess up."

"I sing."

"That's what's up. I knew it. I…"

"You what?"

"Nothing. I was just going to say that I think you need to do something with that."

"I don't know. We'll see."

"You sounded like you could blow to me."

"What do you mean, you've never heard me sing?"

He stared at me for a second. "I don't need to. You and I are dream makers, and dream makes don't need confirmation of their abilities from anyone. You gotta believe that, am I right?"

"I guess."

"Nah baby, you gotta rock that belief. I mean like believe it so much and so hard, you can feel it in your gut. That's the type of belief, I'm talking about. Shoot, I can feel it in my toes. You want me to take my shoes off so you can see?"

I burst out laughing. "I believe you."

"All right now, because I can take these bad boys off in a minute."

"Seriously, I believe you."

His face grew serious. "You know Lorraine, when I left that house, I had nothing but the clothes on my back and this backpack stuffed with a few shirts that I spent too much money on at the bus station's gift shop."

"I was the same way."

He gave me a funny look. "We seem to have a lot in common, huh?"

"We do.".

"Lorraine, do you remember when I told you that my step-father nearly beat me to death?"

"Yeah, you said that your mother saved you."

"She did. I just didn't tell you how."

I turned toward him. "How? How did she save you?"

"She shot him."

I placed my hand on my chest. "Are you serious?"

"I am."

"Did she kill him?"

"No. The bullet grazed his skin, wounding him some, but that was all. It was the only way she could get him off me."

"What did he do?"

"He screamed and cussed at her, but he didn't hit her. He just sat there on the floor holding his leg. That's why I was able to get out of the house."

"I'm glad she didn't kill him."

"I'm not."

"Don't say that."

"It's the truth. I was half-tempted to grab hold of that gun, but I knew that the police would have just seen a black boy that shot a white man, instead of the truth."

I leaned back in my seat.

"Do you think I'm a bad person because I wanted to kill him?"

I could see the sadness in his eyes. "No, I don't. My step-mother used to do horrible things to me, so I know what's it's like to want to return the unkindness."

"That's a nice way of putting it."

"It's the only way I can. The truth is too hard to even talk about."

"Yeah, I get that. Can I tell you something else?"

"Of course."

"I like you. I mean, I know you're a white girl and all, but that doesn't matter to me. It's like you're more like me. Meaning, we seem to have a lot in common."

"Not all white people are like your stepfather."

"You said that your stepmother was."

"True, but my father wasn't. He wasn't perfect. Far from it. He had his vices that caused him to forget for awhile."

"Forget what?"

"That he was a father."

"Did you ever know your real mother?"

"I guess I'd have to determine the definition of a 'real mother' before answering that question."

"Shoot, I think my own mother is still looking for that definition." He said as he finally closed his eyes.

TWENTY-EIGHT

I watched the sun come up. I watched it stretch out its arms and cover New York. Out the window, as the bus moved closer in, I could see the early risers. They walked fast as if they were trying to catch up with life. Some appeared as if they were trying to outrun it.

Women wore gym shoes with stockings and suit skirts. Men had on dark suits with white shirts and skinny dress ties. They carried newspapers under their arms and coffee in their hands.

Cabs were everywhere.

I tapped David on the shoulder to wake him up, and he glanced over and looked out the window.

"It's not like I imagined."

"What did you imagine?" I asked.

"I don't know. I guess I thought it would be lit up with lights or something."

"It's not Las Vegas."

"What do you know about Las Vegas?"

"I know that it's lit up with lights."

We both laughed.

"We're going to make it Lorraine. I can feel it. I can feel my toes tingling. You know what I look forward to the most?"

"What?"

"It's not the fame or the money, it's seeing his face. My stepfather. I want him to see that he was wrong. I don't care if he never apologizes, I doubt that I would accept it if he did, but, I want him to acknowledge that he was wrong. That's what I can't wait for."

He turned towards me.

"I also can't wait to see my little brother again. To hold him in my arms and see that look on his face. The look of peace."

He took my hand as the bus came to a stop.

"Come on, let's go make our dreams happen."

TWENTY-NINE

They say that there is no such thing as love at first sight. They say it is attractiveness. Perhaps even infatuation. But love they say, love takes time.

Mrs. D had not prepared me. She had not prepared for the time I was yearning to give a certain young man. A man who now stood in front of me in a tailored, slim-fitted, two-button black suit coat, gray vest, cuffed black trousers, a white shirt that had the first three buttons from the collar, opened, and freshly-polished black leather shoes. His curly blonde hair was slicked back, and a pair of sunglasses sat in perfect harmony on the brim of his nose.

Yes, I was willing to give him my time, and I prayed that he would not give it back.

His name was Kevin.

I could feel his eyes upon me, resting on my uncomfortable smile as he walked over toward David and me.

"You must be Lorraine." He reached for my suitcase. The one that was being gripped by my left hand. The hand that felt his fingers glide across it.

"You ready to go or do you have more luggage that we're waiting for?"

I searched for my voice. The one that I saw running down the street butt-naked.

Finally, I nodded my head slowly, but it was David's voice that was heard as he held out a piece of paper towards me. “This my cell number. I don’t have a lot of minutes on it, but call me when you get in so we can keep in touch. I’ll purchase some more minutes, as soon as I can.”

I took it and placed it in my pocket.

“We’ll keep in touch, right Lorraine?”

My voice had finally found its way back. “Yes, of course. We promised. I promised.”

He smiled, but he didn’t look to reassured.

I touched his hand. “I promise. I’ll call you as soon as I get in. Let me know where you are staying.”

His face relaxed. “I will.”

He leaned over and kissed me.

THIRTY

There are a lot of things one sees in a rearview mirror as they are driving along. The way our eyes met, was one of them. Seeing my future was another.

"You must be quite a friendly person?"

"Why do you say that?"

"First, you meet Mrs. D, who by the way, has me leaving a busy day at the store to pick you up, and then there's your boyfriend, who I'm assuming you also met on the bus."

"David? He's just a friend."

"Mrs. D, I'm sure is your friend now, but I doubt she kissed you like that before she left."

"He was just saying goodbye, I guess."

I saw him grin.

"I'd say he thinks much differently about your relationship than you do."

"I doubt it."

"You must not know..."

"Know what?"

"How beautiful you are."

I reached down and grabbed my knees so he wouldn't hear them shaking.

"So, you're from Chicago. Went to Maywood High School and graduated second in your class. Got a scholarship, but didn't go to College. I didn't find any work history, so I assume you have never had a job."

"How do you know all that?"

"I looked you up. I had too."

"Really?"

"Of course. Look, don't take offense, but Mrs. D has one of the biggest hearts I've ever seen. She thinks it's her personal responsibility to rescue everyone she deems in trouble or in need. Most of us that work for her either aged out of foster care or were found living on the streets."

"I would have never thought you were either."

"Don't let the suit fool you. If it weren't for Mrs. D, I'd still be living on the street. She took me in after high school and gave me a job. When you turn eighteen and haven't been adopted, the foster care system certainly doesn't waste any time getting you out of their system."

"Mrs. D, thinks highly of you. She talked about you a lot." I replied.

He glanced at me again. Every time our eyes met, I had to admit, there was something there.

"I'd do just about anything for her. All of us that work for her would. It's a shame what happened to her husband. I couldn't believe he was messing around on Mrs. D, like that. Of course, she blames herself."

"Yes, it was a shame. Mrs. D is nice. Blunt, but nice."

He laughed. "Yeah, Mrs. D doesn't beat around the bush, she tells it like it is. I knew her husband was messing around with her, but I didn't have the heart to tell her. Even the smartest, no nonsense kind of women, don't always take to kindly to the truth, especially when it affects them that deeply. It's weird how they can balance the mess out of their bank account, but can't balance their own lives."

"I'm sure, she wouldn't agree with you."

"Actually, I think she would. I even suspect that deep down she knew."

"Can you tell me about the computer program you guys are using?"

"Nice change of subject. I get it. No worries. Just trying to get to know you, that's all, but we'll have plenty of time for that later. I'll drop you off at the apartment and then pick you up this evening for dinner."

"You mean... like a date?"

"I mean, like dinner, unless you're going to get with your boyfriend, what's his name again?"

"David. But I told you that he's not my boyfriend."

"Good. Just wanted to be sure."

I could see him smiling.

Man, he has a smile.

THIRTY-ONE

"We're here."

Kevin unlocked the door, but my body wouldn't move. I stared at the nineteen-story building, afraid to get out. It was beautiful. My thoughts traveled back to a row of small homes in Maywood, Illinois. Our home had two bedrooms, one bathroom, a small kitchen, a family area and a hallway. The furniture was used. The wallpaper was old and peeling. The carpet needed cleaning, and our back porch was falling apart and in desperate need of painting. But we always had food, heat in the winter and portable fans for the summer heat. We had clothes on our backs. In fact, if it hadn't of been for Ole big bones and my daddy being drunk all the time, I wouldn't have had much to complain about.

"It's hard, isn't it?" Kevin asked.

"What do you mean?"

"To walk into a place like that. I remember the first time Mrs. D, brought me here. I sat in the car just like you're doing. I didn't feel as if I were worthy. I remember her grabbing me by the hand and almost dragging me inside."

"You lived here?"

"For about a year, before getting my own place. It's nothing like this one, mine is minuscule, in comparison, but everything in it, except the walls, belongs to me. I've been there for nine years, and I can't explain to you what that feels like. Not too many twenty-eight-year-olds can afford an apartment of their own. Especially not in New York."

He got out the car, opened my door and grabbed my hand. "It will be okay. I promise."

I squeezed his hand, and we walked up to the entrance. The doormen smiled at me as he opened it.

"Everyone here knows Mrs. D, and they respect her. They respect what she does for people like me, like you."

The elevator took us to the nineteenth floor.

"Mrs. D's, apartment is the last one on the right."

"Where are you going?"

"I have to go move the car or else they will tow it. I'll grab your suitcase. Go on, I promise that nothing in there will bite, except Ms. M."

I stood in front of the door. Scared out of my mind to even touch the door knob. As soon as I finally mustered up the nerves, the door flew open, and a short woman with her hair in a bun stood in front of me.

"Child, I ain't got all day for you to stand there staring at the door. Come on."

I stepped back.

She grabbed my hand and pulled me inside.

"I'm Melinda, but all the kids call me Ms. M. I'm the feisty old southern woman, I'm sure Mrs. D told you about. You must be Lorraine."

She looked me over. "Mrs. D was right, you do look like Semeerah."

She placed her hands on her hips. "Anyway, I've got to get my chicken in the oven, I hope you like chicken 'cause that's what I'm cooking for your supper. Where is your suitcase or don't you have one? It's okay if you don't, most of the kids that come here, don't have one. You ain't the first."

"I've got her suitcase Ms. M, and I'm taking her out for dinner tonight."

I turned around and saw Kevin standing there.

"You are huh? That's a first. I ain't never seen you do anything but work since..."

"Ms. M, please don't go there."

"Well, it's the truth. Anyway, you should have called and told me about your dinner plans."

"I'm sorry."

"No mine, she can eat it tomorrow or are you planning on taking her out on another date tomorrow as well?"

"It's just dinner, Ms. M."

"Sure, and I'm young and as beautiful as she is."

"But you are."

"Boy, go put that child's suitcase in the guest bedroom and stop your lying."

He winked at me and walked down the hallway.

She grabbed my hand again and pulled me into what I gathered was the living room. "You better watch out for him."

"Ma'am?"

"His heart ain't been right since..."

"Since what?"

"Nothing. Forget I done said anything. You know how us old women sometimes get, always running off at the mouth. Sometimes, I have to tell my own self to keep quiet."

She looked down the hallway. "Child don't pay me no mine, let me tell you about Mrs. D's place. There are four bedrooms here. The big one is Mrs. D's of course, and the one next to it, is Semeerah's, although she doesn't need it anymore since she ran off and got herself married."

She glanced down the hallway again. "Young people. Young and dumb., I kept telling Mrs. D. However, I suppose that certain truths can make a person do stupid things. That's also what I told Mrs. D, so she wouldn't take it so hard. Anyway, my room is the one on the left. The one by the guest bathroom is yours. I run a tight schedule. You'll be responsible for making your own bed and keeping your room neat. I ain't cleaning up after grown folks, well, except Mrs. D. She the boss, so she can make a mess if she wants to. She never does of course. Most time, it just me here. I clean pretty much everything else. When I cook supper, I usually start around four o'clock. Mrs. D loves my cooking. I think that's the only reason why she keeps an old woman like me around. You better learn how to fry you some good southern chicken. It'll always pay your bills. My mama taught me that. Of course, most young things like you, don't know about cooking. Too busy being cute."

"I know how to cook."

"I'd have to see it to believe it. I ain't met no white woman that know how to really throw down in the kitchen. Shoot, us black women, were throwing down in the kitchen while most of you white women were playing bridge or something. Let me see your hands."

I held my hands out to her.

"Well, you defiantly ain't no stranger to hard work. That be for sure. You might know a little something, something, but like I said, I'd have to see it to believe it." She placed her hands on her chest. "Child, I forgot what I was talking about before we started chatting about cooking. You don't remember either, do you?"

"You were saying that you start cooking dinner around four o'clock."

"That's right. I don't like to get up early either. Despite what everybody says, not all old people get up at the crack of dawn, so you'll have to get your own breakfast, which shouldn't be a problem since you'll be at work by then anyway. Just remember, if you're gonna miss dinner, call me, so I don't tire myself out. I'd rather be watching *Oprah*. You understand?"

"Yes, ma'am."

"Now, I guess I need to tell you about the rules. How old you be again?

"I'm twenty-three."

"Good, so you're grown, but just remember that I'm the real adult around here. I need you in this apartment by one. If you gonna be out later than that, call me, I ain't got time to be waiting up all night. I cut my light out after *The Tonight Show*, but, my ears still hear everything, you understand?"

"I understand."

"Good. You seem like a good young woman, are you?".

"Yes, ma'am."

She gave me a mother's side-eye look.

"Yeah, you are. I can tell. Mrs. D will tell you, I got a knack for spotting troublemakers. I can be twenty-feet away, but they all smell the same to me."

Kevin walked up and stood beside me.

"Isn't that right Kevin?"

"Isn't what right, Ms. M?"

"I was telling Lorraine here, how I got a knack for spotting troublemakers."

She looked directly at him, but when he didn't respond, she turned her attention back to me. "I feel like I forgot something. Oh yes, the most important thing...no men. Period. Don't think you can sneak them in while I'm sleeping. I can hear everything. I might be old, but my hearing is as sharp as your own. Probably even better."

"Ms. M, I think she understands what 'no men,' means?"

They exchanged a look.

"Child, don't be getting sassy with me just because you like her."

Annoyed, he turned toward me. "So, you'll be ready by six?"

"Where are we going?"

"There's a little Italian restaurant not far from the boutique. You do like Italian, right?"

"Sure."

"Great. I'll make reservations for us at seven-thirty. We'll stop by the boutique for a quick tour, and then we'll head there."

"Give the girl a chance to unpack and lay her head down for a few hours."

She looked at her watch. "It's already after four. I know her bones got to be tired from all that riding on the bus."

"Be ready by six. I'll be downstairs waiting on you." He glanced at Ms. M, daring her to say anything else.

"Go on child, get yourself unpacked before mister bossy here, changes it to 5. You remember which room is yours?"

"Yes, ma'am."

"Good," she said, as she walked away.

"Do you have a skirt and a nice blouse for tonight?" Kevin asked.

"I have a few things that Mrs. D purchased for me."

"I'll see them when I pick you up. If need be, we'll get you something beautiful from the boutique, okay?"

"Okay."

"Get rid of the ponytail. I'm sure you'll look even more amazing with your hair down, don't you agree?"

He stepped in front of me. "Can I join David's club?"

"What club is that?"

"The club where I get to kiss you."

Ms. M poked her head from around the corner. "I can't believe you didn't just tell her you were going to do it. You seem to be telling her how to do everything else."

He ignored her and placed a kiss on my cheek.

"I'll see you at six o'clock, sharp."

I watched him leave. His cologne still lingering in the air. For the first time in my life, I felt like skipping about. I felt like..."

"Just remember what I told you, child," Ms. M shouted, before disappearing back around the corner.

THIRTY-TWO

Taupe walls. Beautiful cream sheets. Silk pillows that completely covered the top of the bed. A rich gold chair that sat in the corner. A nightstand made out of glass. Plush cream carpet from one end of the room, clear to the other.

It all took my breath away.

As I stood there, my thoughts couldn't help but think about Ella. The tears began to form in the corners of my eyes. I was standing in the most amazing bedroom that I had ever seen, and I knew, I knew that Ella was sitting in her squeaking bed wishing I was there by her side.

My heart wanted to run. Run back to Chicago and wrap my arms around her. Protect her as I promised.

Promises.

I remember my mother telling me when I was five years old, that promises are either kept or broken. The moment we make them, she said, we have already determined the outcome in our hearts.

I reached into my pocket and pulled out David's phone number.

"Hello."

"David, it's Lorraine."

"I didn't think you would really call."

"I promised that I would. I don't have much time to talk."

"Why? What's going on? You okay?"

"No, no, it's nothing like that. I just have to get dressed, Kevin is taking me to the boutique for a tour and then we're going out to dinner."

"He doesn't waste any time, does he?"

"What's that supposed to mean."

"I saw him checking you out at the bus station. I saw you checking him out as well, or was that just in my imagination?"

"It's just dinner. Did you find a place to stay yet?"

"Actually, I did. You wouldn't believe it, but I also got a gig."

"A what?"

"A gig. A job. Boy, you need some schooling."

"Whatever. How did you do that so fast?"

"I told you, I believe in me. I know what I can do."

"What sort of job did you get?"

"Playing the piano in this jazz club not too far from the bus station. I saw the sign, walked in, and after playing a few notes, the owner gave me the job. The place is called— The Skinny. It's a real cool joint. Very upscale. The owner's name is Misty."

"You never mentioned that you could play the piano."

"My mother made me start taking lessons when I was just a kid. I've been playing for over nineteen years. Truth be told, I always hated playing the piano, but my mother would never allow me to give it up. Anyway, the owner has a small apartment over the club that she's letting me crash in until I can get a place on my own. From the way I heard it, this place is jumping off on the weekends, so it shouldn't take me long."

"Wow, I'm impressed. You're already in the music industry."

"Playing the piano wasn't in my plan, but it will do for now. I'm learning that my plans don't always work out the way I had them play out in my mind, but it's cool."

"When do you start?"

"This weekend. Here's the other thing, Misty used to own one of the biggest record labels in New York. I mean like, the woman knows the industry. She's got mad connections."

"You sound excited."

"I am, but I'm going to keep my cool. This is New York and people in the music industry always play themselves up to be more than they really are. I'm going to ask around tomorrow and check her out. So are you going to come and hear me play on Friday? You don't start your computer gig until next week, right?"

"Monday. I'm nervous. "

"Don't be. You seem pretty darn smart to me, so believe in that and run like the wind with that piece of knowledge about yourself."

"I didn't realize you were so encouraging. I'm going to have to call you anytime I feel down?"

"You felt it too huh?"

I knew what he meant. "Yeah. This place is amazing David. It really is, but, I miss her, and I feel..."

"Guilty?"

"Exactly. What if we turn out to have this amazing life, while they suffer? The thought tears me apart. It makes me want to just go back. Deal with whatever my step-mother comes at me with, just so I can protect Ella. I never told you all the stuff she did to Ella and me—me especially."

"Just remember that we're doing all of this for them. I will go back and get my little brother, just like I know you will go and get your little sister. We made them a promise, and we either live or die by our promises."

"Where did you get that saying about promises from? It's something I heard growing up."

"I don't know. I think I read it somewhere a long time ago and it just stuck with me. Look, Lorraine, we're here. Don't lose focus."

"I have to go. I've got to get dressed."

"For your date with the suited-up white boy."

"It's just dinner and his name is Kevin, remember?"

"I wish I could forget. Believe that. Anyway, I gotta go as well, my minutes are about to run out on this phone anyway. I haven't gotten a chance to purchase more of them. I'm going to try and not think about you and 'Kevin' tonight...having 'just' dinner. Don't be surprised if I turn up at the restaurant. Where did you say he was taking you?"

"Some Italian restaurant. He didn't say the name."

"Where are you staying at anyway?"

"I'll have to get the address from Ms. M, she's the housekeeper, but the boutique is called Dena Fox. It's on Fifth Avenue, I think."

"I remember her mentioning that on the bus."

"What do you mean, you weren't on the bus with us?"

The line went dead.

I glanced at the clock. It was 5:20.

Mrs. M, knocked on the door just as I went to open my suitcase.

"I thought maybe you'd like to wear this tonight."

She held up a beautiful long and flowing black skirt that looked as if it was made out of very expensive silk.

"It goes with this here cream blouse. You'll have to wear a camisole underneath it, the sequins will rub your skin off under the arms, and you'll be cussing me about it."

"They are both so beautiful. I couldn't."

"Of course their beautiful child, Mrs. D made them. Semeerah wore them once for an interview with Vogue Magazine. You are her be about the same size and height, so I thought you could wear them tonight."

"I don't even own a camisole."

"I'll go see if there is one in Semeerah's old room. That child had more clothes than even she knew what to do with. When she got married, she left them all here."

"Why? They're so beautiful."

"You'll have to ask Mrs. D about that. It ain't like me to tell other people's secrets." She placed them on my bed and glanced at her watch. "You better hurry child, Kevin can be Kevin."

"What does that mean?"

"Keep him waiting, and you'll see. Now hurry up and shower. You'll find everything you need in the bathroom. There are fresh towels in the cabinet under the sink. I'll run and get the camisole."

I was showered and zipping up the skirt by the time Ms. M came back into the room.

"Sorry child, I had a hard time finding this thing." She handed me the camisole and looked at my feet. "What about shoes, child? What size you be?"

"I wear a size eight."

"I'll be back."

Five minutes later, Ms. M came back with a pair of heels that scared me to even think about walking in.

"What's wrong child, you ain't never seen stilettos before?"

"I've seen them; I just have never walked in a pair before."

"Child, Semeerah wore these types of shoe all the time. That girl wouldn't put her feet in anything less than five inches. I think she was wearing four-inch heels by the time she was thirteen. Try them on. You'll be fine. Just take baby steps until you get a feel for them. It doesn't take rocket science to wear heels."

I took the shoes from her and slipped them on. "For me, it just might."

She watched me stumble around the room for a few minutes. "Don't kill yourself in them things. Be careful."

I stood in front of her, trying to steady myself in the shoes. "Do I look okay?"

She glanced me up and down. "You look exactly the way I thought you would. Now get on downstairs, Kevin be here in a few minutes."

THIRTY-THREE

At exactly six, Kevin pulled up.

The moon glanced down at him. The stars turned in our direction, and my knees started to rattle as I stood there taking him in.

The black suit had been replaced with a navy one. The gray vest was now a blue-stripped one. He still had on the open-collar white shirt and brown leather shoes. His curly hair enhanced the look. When he moved toward me, I got lost in a world where cathedral-length wedding gowns and sculptured lilies bloomed. I could hear soft music and see first dances. I could feel gentle kisses and three letter words dripping from our lips. Words that I had never tasted before. Until now.

He paused when he reached me. "What do you have on?"

The tone of his voice took me by surprise. "What's wrong? Don't you like it? Ms. M gave it to me."

"Those belong to Semeerah, Ms. M, knew better."

"You think Semeerah would get angry? I'm sorry, I can run back up and change, I had no idea."

"She wouldn't get angry." His voice softened as he noticed the tears welling up in the corners of my eyes. "I'm sorry." He grabbed my hand and kissed it. His lips were warm. "You look amazing. You really do. I didn't mean to come at you like that. The clothes just threw me off, that's all. Remember, I told you that I use to pick out some of Semeerah's outfits. She wore that one for a magazine interview."

"Yes, Ms. M told me. It was for Vogue."

"I'm sure she did."

He smiled.

It was a slow, sweet smile that touched every forgiving part of me.

"We're going to be late if we don't get a move on it, and I want to take you to the boutique before heading to the restaurant." He touched my hair just as he opened the car door and I slid in.

"I knew it would look beautiful down."

I thought he was going to lean over and kiss me, but he closed the door.

THIRTY-FOUR

Kevin stood off to the side as I took it all in. From beautiful long beaded gowns to shoes with plenty of sparkles, Mrs. D's, boutique had me feeling like a little girl wanting to play dress up.

The walls were draped in a shimmering cream wallpaper. The crystal chandeliers made them come to life when the light hit them. The dark and rich-looking mahogany floors were spotted with thick and plush white rugs. Pearls and glass were everywhere the eyes traveled.

Kevin was like a proud father as he paraded me down each row of dresses. I could tell he was proud of every piece that hung from the custom pearl-wrapped hangers.

"Every single gown was designed by Mrs. D. We're one of the top boutiques in New York. We even get celebrities that come here to find gowns for their special events. Since our gowns are all one-of-a-kind, they love it. They are beautiful aren't they?"

He came toward me.

I braced myself as he wrapped his hands around my waist. "Do you want to try one on?" He whispered in my ear.

"Okay," I replied.

He stepped back. "Pick one."

"I wouldn't know which one to pick."

He pulled one off the hanger and handed it to me. It was a gorgeous empire-waist, deep blue gown with heavy silver beading and a slightly low back. "Any of them would look beautiful on you. Trust me." He pointed toward the dressing room.

When I stepped out of the dressing room, he handed me a pair of silver shoes with a low heel. "You ready to go dancing?"

"I thought we were going to the Italian restaurant?"

"We are, but they have an amazing space for dancing that's connected to the restaurant."

"You don't think this is too much for an Italian restaurant?"

"It's not your typical Italian restaurant, you'll see."

"Kevin."

He stopped and turned toward me.

"Why were you really offended by the clothes that Ms. M, gave me to wear tonight? Did you and Semeerah date or something? Were you in love with her?"

He walked over toward me.

"I didn't care for the clothes because I knew Mrs. M, only gave them to you to be spiteful and I hated to see you put in the middle of our dislike for each other. I shouldn't have reacted the way I did, I'm sorry. It won't happen again."

"Ms. M, thinks Semeerah and I look alike, what do you think?"

"You do."

"Is that why you're attracted to me?"

He pulled me to him, and our eyes found their resting place in each others'. "I'm not going to lie, Lorraine, you do look so much like her, except for the skin color, of course. But, I'm not attracted to you because of that. I know Ms. M might think so. It's a long story about her and me, but please believe me when I say that when I look at you, I only see you. Not Semeerah. You're smart and beautiful. I don't think you even know how much." He pulled away, and his eyes felt as if they were sinking down into me. "Are you attracted to me?"

The answer to his question came with an easiness that scared me. The two words slipped off my tongue and landed in his hands. It was up to him to determine what to do with them.

"I am."

"I know we just met and we have a lot to learn about each other, but I want to be clear about one thing...I want to be your man. I knew it the moment you got off that bus. I'm not going to beat around the brush about that, and I'm not going to play games. I want you to understand my intentions moving forward. I'm not like most twenty-eight-year-old men, just out here looking for one thing. That's not me. I know what it's like to have nothing and now that I'm where I am, I want everything...starting with you."

He moved quickly, scooping me up and nestling me into his arms. Our lips enjoyed a moment together.

"Ms. M told me I should be careful when it comes to you. Was she right?"

He pulled away slowly. "Absolutely," he replied, as he clicked off the lights. "Let's go."

THIRTY-FIVE

The La'Bre boasted a solid mix of a high-end clientele, expensive wine, gourmet Italian dishes that are cooked in the center of the restaurant, and a beautiful dance room with carefully crafted Italian marble floors.

The music the dance room featured ranged from Italian dance classics to Michael Jackson. I watched as women checked in their thousand dollar shoes and hit the dance floor barefooted. Guys had removed their ties and suit jackets which were neatly hung together, on a wall toward the back of the dance room.

"This place is fantastic," I said, over the music.

"I know. I love coming here. I can only do so, once or twice a year. The food here is just as amazing as the dancing, don't you think?"

I nodded my head, as I placed a fork full of the white wine cream pasta dish that sat before me.

"Some of them on the floor tonight are from the World's leading dance companies. In fact, some of the top Broadway dancers come here after their last performance. I came here when I can, just to see them perform. It's like getting a free show."

"How did you find this place?"

"Mrs. D. She makes everyone who works for her, go to the theater. This was how I did it so I could save my money."

"What are you saving for?"

He placed his fork down. "I'm going to open my own men's clothing store. It will specialize in custom-tailored suits and one-of-a-kind ties. I made the suit and tie I have on."

"Does Mrs. D, know? I mean, won't you be in competition with her?"

"No, she specializes in women's clothing only, and yes, she knows. I wouldn't even have the determination to pursue it if it weren't for her encouraging me to do so."

"When do you think you will open it?"

"There's a cool vacant shop about a block or two from the bus station that I've been eyeing. It's not high-end like Mrs. D's, I can't afford that starting out, but that area is still decent, and it will be something to call my own."

"It is by this jazz club called The Skinny?"

"It is. How do you know it?"

"I'm going there on Friday to hear David perform. He got a job there. He calls it a gig."

"He got a job that quick?"

"He did."

"What kind of gig is it?"

"He's playing the piano."

"So, he's got talent. Good for him."

"It is. He's determined to make it in the music industry. He really wants to be a manager, but like he said, playing the piano, for now, pay the bills."

"The music industry is not for everyone, and there's more than a dozen people in New York that can play the piano."

"I'm sure, but I'm still happy for him."

"I can tell."

"Some lady named Misty who owns the place hired him. David seemed to think that she was once pretty big in the music industry."

"If Misty hired him personally, he must be an exceptional piano player, not just a good one. She's tough. She initially passed on Semeerah."

"Really? That's hard to believe."

"Well, hard to believe it may be, but she did. She said her voice wasn't strong enough."

"David said he's been playing the piano for nineteen years, started when he was five."

"You seem to know a lot about him."

"It was a long bus ride."

He chuckled. "That's true."

"So, do you know this Misty? Is she really that well-known in the music Industry?"

"Mrs. D knows her pretty well, and yes, Misty is well-known in the music industry. Has been for years."

"I know he will be happy to hear that."

"A lot of very famous music artists got their start at her club. She's owned that place for years. I think it used to be her father's or something like that. There were a lot of rumors about her, back in the day, but I will say that if David is playing there, he's in the right spot, that's for sure."

"I still can't believe she turned down Semeerah. I know she wishes she hadn't."

"Semeerah is doing good, that's true, but she'd be doing better if she had a record label as strong as Misty's. I guess that's why she's trying to start her own."

"I hope I get to meet her one day?"

"Misty?"

"No, Semeerah. Mrs. D said she was going to call her and ask her to come to New York so that she and I could meet."

"Why?"

"Mrs. D thinks that Semeerah can help me."

"With what?"

"I want to sing." "Is that really what you want to do, sing for a living."

"Why say it like that?"

"I think you would do so much better without it."

"Why?"

"Like I said before, and I meant it, you're smart. You've got brains and believe it or not, those can take you so much further than a music contract can. Mrs. D tried to get Semeerah to go to college or learn some skill, but all she wanted to do was sing. She's making money now, but, one day that will end, then what?"

"So you don't think I should pursue singing?"

"I know I can't tell you what to do, but, I hope that you don't go down that path. You will never have a real life. You will always be in the spotlight."

"Is that what happened to Semeerah? Is that why you and she didn't work?"

The waiter came over and took our plates.

He waited for the waiter to leave. "I see Ms. M got in your ear with her foolishness."

"Why don't you like her, Ms. M, I mean?"

"She thought there was more to Semeerah and me than there was and she drew conclusions about things and didn't bother to get all the facts."

"She seems sweet to me."

"Ask her why she gave you Semeerah's clothes to put on, then tell me how sweet she really is."

"I see."

"I hope you do." He stood up and extended his hand. "Shall we join them?"

"Out there? I don't actually dance."

Kevin led me to the dance floor. A young lady came up and asked for my shoes. Kevin removed his jacket and vest and handed both to her.

The music started. The song was slow and engaging as Kevin moved me around the dance floor.

"So, is David my competition?" He asked, as he gently twirled me and then brought back in close to him.

"Like I told you before, he's a friend. Is Semeerah mine?"

"You're the only one in my arms, aren't you?"

"But is she in your heart?"

He stopped. "You're the only one there as well."

THIRTY-SIX

There I was on the street, staring at this lady. The bag lady. As she turned around, I saw not her face, but my own.

In one bag, there was my responsibility to Ella. I had it wrapped around my wrist, holding on to it like my life depended on it.

I opened up the other bag, and I saw her. My birth mother. I couldn't see her face, but I could see her heart. It was in my bag, beating.

Then there was the bag that seemed to be the heaviest. I opened it up, and black balloons emerged. They surrounded me. I could see myself beginning to drift upward. I was floating over New York. Floating back to Chicago. I could see our home.

Old Big Bones stood on the porch. She looked up, and when saw me, she threw something in the air, causing my balloons to pop. Next thing I knew I was falling. Dying, and she was smiling. Smiling as she watched me hit the ground.

I could hear his voice. Kevin's voice. He was telling me to get up. When I looked into his eyes, I saw someone there. Someone staring back at me.

It was Semeerah.

She was knocking on my door.

"Lorraine, child, you up?"

I jumped at the sound of Ms. M, knocking on my door. My heart pounding. Tears in my eyes.

"You okay, child?" She opened the door and come inside.

"I'm okay, just a bad dream." I slowly responded.

"I made some coffee, whole wheat toast, and bacon."

"I thought you didn't make breakfast."

She glanced at the computer manual for the boutique that lay on top of my comforter.

"You know that thing yet?"

"It's been my constant morning companion, these last few days."

"I noticed. It seems Kevin has been your evening one. What time did you come in last night? Y'all go dancing again at that fancy restaurant?"

"No, and Ms. M you know exactly when I put that key in the front door."

She smiled. "You be right about that. I just hope you're still a 'good' girl with all this wining and dining he doing with ya."

"We go out to dinner, we go for walks, we talk. Nothing else."

She gave me the once over. "I was just checking," she said, as she placed her hands on her hips. "You know the boutique is sponsoring that big charity event tonight, you going?"

"Ms. M, it's Friday. You know I'm going to see my friend David tonight at that jazz club I told you about."

"Kevin seemed to be calling all the shots each day, so I wasn't sure if he was letting you go."

"I'm going."

"Um-hum. We'll see."

"I promised David that I would come, so I'm going."

"Like I said, we'll see."

"I wonder why Mrs. D hasn't called?"

Her face grew sad. "You know the funeral is this Saturday. I'm sure she be back in Chicago by now. Don't worry, she'll come when she can. You know women aren't like men, it takes time for us to conquer the pain."

"Do you think Semeerah is going to the funeral?"

"Ask Kevin."

"What really went on with them? I know you know."

She came and sat on my bed. "What did he tell ya?"

"He said that they were close friends and that he loved her, but not in that way. Not like a girlfriend or something."

"At least he has the or 'something' right?"

"Were they more than that?"

"I think he wanted it to be, but Semeerah was young. When she turned twenty-one, I think he thought she would grow up. But truth be told, that child never really did. She's still a child in so many ways. The music industry spoiled her, Mrs. D, spoiled her and..."

"You spoiled her?"

"I did. I ain't gonna have no regrets about that."

"Why did you give me Semeerah's clothes to put on?"

"I wanted you to see his reaction. Let me tell you something child, and you listen real good."

I sat up in my bed.

"A man's actions will tell you everything you need to know about him. Not his words."

"Ms. M, why don't you like Kevin?"

"I don't like bullies. They become violent. I know the type. My ex-husband used to put his hands on me, and he didn't have to be drunk. It was in his blood. His daddy used to beat his mother. No different than Kevin's old man. How do you think he ended up in foster care?

"He doesn't talk about it, but I got the impression that something appalling happened to him."

"His daddy killed his mama right in front of him. Beat the poor child to death. Why you think Kevin has control issues?"

"I don't know."

"He told me that as he stood there, holding his mother, he felt like everything that happened that day, he had no control over. Like he was powerless. I know how he felt. I know what it's like to not have control over things that happen to you. My ex, he took my child."

"What do you mean?"

"I mean that he had done beat me so bad one day, I lost it."

"I'm so sorry Ms. M."

"That was forty something years ago. I guess that's why I spoiled Semeerah. She was like my own child. Mrs. D left her in my care most of the time. Mrs. D stayed in Chicago and Semeerah stayed her with me until she signed that record deal when she was twelve-years-old. Kevin come through those doors a year later. He was around eighteen, fresh out of high school, discharged out of the foster care system and determined."

"How did he and Mrs. D, come to know each other?"

"He doesn't tell you much, I see."

"We talk."

"Not about anything important, it seems. Mrs. D was here visiting Semeerah and helping her get ready for her first music tour. Kevin walked into her boutique and told her that she needed to hire him as her in-house seamstress. He didn't have any experience, so at first, Mrs. D turned him down. But then, one day she saw him living on the street. She asked him if he really knew how to sew. Believe it or not, that man can sew his butt off."

"That I did know."

"Well, good for you. Anyway, it also appeared that he had a knack for bossing people around and Mrs. D's, boutique manager had just left, without giving notice. So, instead of hiring Kevin to be a seamstress, she hired him to run the boutique. I admit, he's mighty good at it. Kevin was everything Mrs. D needed for the boutique and she trusts him. Too much if you ask me."

"I wonder how come Mrs. D didn't just move here."

"She has a two boutiques in Chicago, plus, her husband didn't want to. He was actually trying to get her to move to Atlanta. Now we all know why. I never liked him. I think he only married Mrs. D for her money, but I'll never admit that I said that, if you should try to use it against me."

"Ms. M, you know I wouldn't."

"Child, they only thing I know is when *Oprah* and *The Price Is Right* come on. Everything and everyone else is suspect."

"You never remarried?"

"There were a few that tried to put a ring on me, but, I wasn't having it. I figure that's the only way to make sure no man can put their hands on me again."

"Kevin, is bossy, but I don't that he would ever hit me or be violent like that."

"You keep thinking that way child. I saw him. I saw him put his hands on Semeerah. I tried to tell her to report it to Mrs. D, but, she just kept it to herself. Said it was nothing. That it was her fault. Let me tell you this child, it ain't never your fault, you hear me? You understand what I'm saying to you?"

I nodded.

She stared into my eyes. "It's too late, isn't it?"

"Too late for what?"

"I can tell he done got to you. Got your nose all up in the air, sniffing his cologne and loving it, so I know you ain't believing me right now. Just know that you don't have to learn the hard way."

I lowered my eyes.

"So, when are you gonna tell me your story? Everybody that walks through those doors got one."

"You know last night as Kevin and I were heading inside the restaurant, I saw this lady. She was homeless, but you could tell that her life was in the bags that she clung to. That's how I feel, Ms. M, like that bag lady. I even had the worst dream about her. Actually, I dreamt that I was her."

She wiped the tears from my eyes. "It's okay child. Why don't you get up and get yourself showered? You'll find some breakfast on the counter."

"Thanks, Ms. M."

"Don't get used to it."

"I'll be there in a few."

She stopped at the door. "So, when you think he's going to ask?"

"Ask what?"

"That question you were thinking about, the moment you saw him."

"I don't know what you mean."

"Sure you do. You forgot I'm almost seventy, I know the look of dumb love."

"Ms. M!"

"Child, you mark my words, that man is gonna ask. I give it six months tops."

"You think?"

"See! I knew you were sprung. Bye child. Get your shower, then eat your breakfast. Don't forget to lay your clothes out for that charity event tonight."

"I told you, I'm going to the jazz club."

"Right and one day I'm going to burn my fried chicken."

THIRTY-SEVEN

I glanced at my clock. It was almost six, and I was still sitting on the bed trying to figure out what to put on. Kevin had given me some clothes from the boutique that he said were from previous seasons that hadn't sold.

My phone rang.

"Lorraine, it's David. You still coming tonight?"

"Of course. What time do you go on?"

"I go on at nine. Are you sure you're going to make it? Please, don't let me down."

"David, I promise you, I will be there."

"Okay, okay. Sorry, I guess, I'm just nervous. Misty said that it's going to be a packed house this evening. This night is so important to me. Everything is riding on it."

"I know you will be great. I hear Misty doesn't hire anyone unless they are exceptional."

"She's something, that I will say. She knows her stuff. I've been practicing all week."'

"You got this, believe in yourself."

"You got jokes, huh?"

"No, I'm just trying to be encouraging, like you were for me."

"I'll be whatever you want me to be Lorraine."

"David..."

"How have you been? I've tried to call you."

"I've been good. This week has been a whirlwind, I've been studying that software manual for the boutique every day."

"That's good, but I don't know why; I thought you wanted to sing."

"This computer job will help pay the bills."

"You know I get that, but, you're not giving up on singing, are you?"

I didn't respond.

"I'll take your silence as a yes, although, I hope not. So how's Kevin? I'm sure you two have been going out on more dinner dates."

"Kevin is good."

"I can't wait to see you, Lorraine, I feel like it's been forever. These last four days have been torture for me. I actually wish we could take another bus trip."

I laughed. "I think I'll pass on sitting on a bus for eighteen hours."

"If it met sitting next to you, I'd do it tomorrow."

"I'll see you in a few."

"You know how to get here?"

"I'm sure the cab driver does. Now, let me go so I can get there on time."

"Okay. You promise you're coming?"

"Kevin!"

"I'm just kidding. I'll see you in a bit."

I slipped into the shower. When I came back out, I heard the phone ringing again.

"David, I'm never going to make it there if you keep calling me."

"It's me, Kevin."

"Kevin, I'm sorry. I thought you were David."

"You seem terribly excited to see him tonight."

"Don't start Kevin, I told you, I promised him that I would come."

"Yeah, I know, that's why I'm coming with you."

"What about the Charity event? Isn't the boutique, one of the sponsors?"

"It sounds like you don't want me to go."

"It's not like that."

"You sure?"

"Of course."

"Good. I'm here at the Charity event now. I'll stay another couple of hours. I called the club, and they said that your friend goes on around nine, so, I should be there by then."

"Okay." I hung up.

I turned around and saw Ms. M standing there.

"Change of plans?"

"No, I'm still going to the club tonight, just as before..."

"But?"

"Kevin is also coming. He's going to stay at the Charity event for another couple of hours, and then he's coming to meet me."

She laughed. "I knew it. He always got to be in control."

"It's okay."

"You keep telling yourself that child. You keep telling yourself that because all you see is a good-looking man taking an interest in ya. I'd bet money, you ain't never had the attention of a man before, and now you done landed the eyes of Mister super-fine Kevin, and don't know how to handle it. Am I right?"

"Ms. M, please. Don't..."

She stared at me. "Fine. I'll keep my mouth shut. I ain't trying to hurt ya feeling child. I'm sorry."

She walked over and gave me a hug. "I just don't want to see you get hurt child. Ms. M takes seriously every child under her care and Mrs. D put you in my care. I didn't do right with Semeerah. I let my guard down, but you best believe it ain't gonna happen again. You go on and have yourself a good time, Ms. M will be here when you get home. I'll hear your key in the door."

"I know you will."

"You know Semeerah is coming?"

I stopped and turned toward her. "She's not going to the funeral?"

"Of course she is, but, she'll be here in two weeks."

"Is she coming alone?"

She looked at me.

"I mean, is she coming with her husband?"

"I don't think so, but who knows with Semeerah. I'd be surprised if that child is still married to him."

"You think Kevin knows she's coming?"

"He's your man, ain't he? Ask him."

THIRTY-EIGHT

The Skinny sat on the corner. Tall brown mahogany doors welcomed you. The poetic mix of horns, saxophones and drums floated into the air each time the security guard allowed someone to enter.

Women wore sequined skirts and sleeveless blouses with pearl necklaces that seemed to drape down to the ground. Not a high heel under five inches could be found.

David had been right; the place was packed. I could see the long lines of people waiting to get in, as my cab pulled up.

It was almost nine. I searched for Kevin. I didn't see him, but I saw David standing by the doorway.

"You made it. I just beginning to think you weren't coming. You look amazing, way different, but in a good way."

"Kevin is coming."

"You serious?"

"Yeah, he said he'd be here by nine, so he should be pulling up in a few."

"Wasn't expecting that, but, I don't blame him. I thought you were beautiful on the bus, but man Lorraine!"

"David stop. It's just the clothes. You look good as well."

"I hope so. I spent just about everything I had left on these."

He did a quick turn. "You like?"

"I do. Very handsome."

"That means a lot coming from you."

He took my hand. "I was really hoping you were coming by yourself, there's something I need to tell you, after the show."

A woman stepped out of the club. "David, It's nine. You're up."

"That's the boss. Let's go. I've got a table ready for you. It's right up front. I'll have them pull up another chair…for Kevin."

"Thank you, David."

"Sure, no problem, I'm just glad you kept your promise."

He learned over and kissed me on the cheek.

"Lorraine."

I turned around and saw Kevin standing there.

The two stared each other down for a few minutes.

"I'll see you inside Lorraine, I have to go. Thanks again for coming, maybe we'll get a chance to talk afterward."

Kevin placed his arm around my waist. "You ready to go inside?"

I turned toward David. "We'll see you inside."

I followed Kevin into the club.

"David has a table ready near the front."

"I've taken care of that."

He gave his name to the hostess and she led us to a section that had a V.I.P. sign in front of it. The rope was removed, and Kevin and I were escorted to a booth.

My eyes traveled the walls that told the story of famous jazz singers. They rested on the candles that lit up the smiling faces of grown folks who snaps their fingers, bobbed their heads and said yes to the vibes of music that proposed to them.

I watched them. Drinking in the rhythm that surrounded them. I saw hands touching on tops of tables, gentle kisses and intimate looks.

The announcer came on the stage, and the lights took their place. His voice drew anticipation as he welcomed David to the stage.

The moment David took the stage, the audience grew silent as soft blue lights followed David to the piano. Their ears enjoyed the romance of his fingers gliding along the keys. The lights dimmed.

The sounds of enchanting melodies echoed through the air. They were slow and intoxicating.

His hands moved with ease.

The music he played filled your lungs as it touched every part inside of you. You could feel it in your toes. It made your hands tingle as it poured out through your fingertips. You were there, traveling from piano key to piano key. It was a journey that you never wanted to end. A moment that you were glad to have witnessed, it's beginning. You could see it floating from table to table. Lingering for moments on some.

When he was done, he stood up, and the audience erupted in applause.

He took a bow, and when he came up, he was looking in my direction. I watched as he stepped up to the announcer's microphone. "I would like to play another song for you tonight, but to do so, I need a little help. See this song is one that, while the piano can give it life, it takes a voice to make you really feel it. There is someone here tonight that has just the voice this song needs. She'll need a little encouragement, so let's show her some New York love as I call her up to the stage tonight. She's a beautiful woman and friend. Ladies and gentlemen, let's welcome my good friend, Lorraine to the stage. You can call her Lady L."

I sat there with my mouth wide open. Kevin looked at me.

The audience began to clap even louder.

Kevin slowly motioned me toward the stage, although I could tell he wasn't happy about it.

The lights followed me as I walked up to David and whispered in his ear. "I don't know what to sing."

"Just start singing, and I'll follow your lead. Don't worry, I got you. Believe."

I gave him a nervous smile.

The lights dimmed again. The audience grew silent.

I closed my eyes, and when I opened my voice, it was as if I were meant to be standing there, at that moment, on that stage.

I could hear David mixing in the piano with my voice. As I sang, I let all my troubles, all my pain, free. I released them and dared them to find me again.

In the darkness, somewhere in the lights, I could see Ella. I could see her smiling at me. She was proud. I reached out toward her and wrapped her in my arms, and as I looked into her eyes, I sang.

When the song was done, I heard them. The audience. I opened my eyes and saw them standing. Every one of them.

THIRTY-NINE

"I'm an old lady, but I know talent."

I stared at the woman that stood in front of me with a cream suit on and diamond jewelry that could light up the club, all on its own. Her rich brown skin was enriched by her salt and pepper hair that laid softly on the cusp of her shoulders. Lean fingers. Perfectly polished nude fingernail polish.

"Yes, David was amazing." I finally manage to utter.

I could feel her eyes taking me in, summing up my insides as if she were determining their worth. Her voice was as smooth as a piano's keystroke.

"That David was, I take nothing away from him. It's why I hired him, but I was referring to you." She extended her hand. "I'm Misty, the Owner."

We shook. Her grip was dominating. "I'm Lorraine, a friend of David's."

"No, you're not."

"Ma'am?"

"You name from this day forward will be known as Lady L, I will make sure of it, that's what I do, and I'm the best at it."

Kevin stepped from around me. "That's kind of you, but Lorraine here, isn't interested in singing, are you Lorraine?" He wrapped his arm around me.

Misty gave him a slow and sly smile. "You work for Dena Fox, I believe. A women's boutique manager. How nice. It is a cute little shop. How is Semeerah?"

"I wouldn't know."

"Sure you don't. Look, when I need a new dress, I'll let you know, but right now, this conversation doesn't involve you. Lady L here is a woman, not a child, she can speak for herself." She turned her attention back toward me. "It was a pleasure to hear you sing tonight. You have a beautiful voice. Use it. That's what it's there for. David will give you my card. We'll be in touch with you."

She walked away, the same way she came up to us. With confidence.

A few seconds later, a lady passing by bumped into Kevin and spilled some of her coke on his pants leg. He pulled away from me. "Excuse me, I'll be back in a second."

David and I watched as he headed toward the men's restroom.

"He doesn't look too happy."

"No, I imagine he's not."

"Misty is right, you were amazing up there Lorraine. Just amazing. I knew you could sing, I mean, I had heard you on the bus, but tonight was simply amazing. We can do amazing things together. We could..."

"What do you mean, you heard me on the bus?"

He glanced in the direction of the restroom, grabbed my hand and then led me out the back door.

"What's going on David?"

"I need to tell you something."

"What is it?"

"I heard you sing Lorraine. I heard you sing on the bus to Atlanta. I was on it. I was sitting behind you and Mrs. Dena Fox."

"How can that be? I would have seen you?"

"I had a hat on, so I don't think you saw me."

"This doesn't make any sense. When we met, you made it seem as if we were meeting for the first time."

"I got off the bus in Michigan when you got off."

"Why?"

"Because, I heard you and Mrs. Fox talking about New York, and I thought that maybe, I would have a better shot in New York than in Atlanta."

"You mean, you thought you would have a better chance with me?"

"Well, yes, but..."

Kevin walked out.

"He's also a thief. Did he tell you that?"

"What is he talking about David?"

"Tell her how you pick-pocketed money from Mrs. D."

I turned toward Kevin. "How do you know that?"

"I spoke to Mrs. D the other day. When I mentioned that you were going to hear some guy tonight that you met on the bus perform, she asked me to describe him. I did. That's when she told me that David here, had bumped into her; when she got on the bus, the money in her coat pocket was gone. All of it."

"Is this true David, is it!"

"Let me explain Lorraine." He stepped toward me, but I stepped back.

"I was just about broke. I only had enough to get my ticket to New York. I knew I would need money once I got here. I saw her handing you some money and then..."

"You thought you could just take it for yourself? How could you? You were supposed to be my friend!"

"I am. I swear. I was going to tell you all of it tonight."

I turned toward Kevin. "Take me home."

"Lorraine, please. Please, Lorraine. I'm sorry. Please."

"Don't ever call me again David." Kevin and I began to walk away.

"I spoke to him, Lorraine. I spoke to Jeffery. I finally got up the nerve to call. He understood. You were right, he understood."

I glared at him. "I remember when you told me that you were determined. Determined to do whatever it took to bring him to you. I never thought that meant that you were determined to hurt me."

"Lorraine, I am sorry. I really am, but don't leave. Misty can help us. She can help us both get where we want to be. We can bring them both to us. We can do it together. Think about Ella."

"Don't you ever say my sister's name." I quickly walked over to him. My anger blazing. "Tell me something David, did you tell Misty that I would perform tonight? Is that the real reason you called? You wanted to be sure I would be here. I bet you arranged all of this in advance because you knew it would help you. Am I right? Don't lie to me David, am I right?"

He nodded. "I had told Misty about you, but, I only did it because I knew how good you were and I knew that you and I wanted the same thing."

"No David, we don't want the same thing. I don't want to use people. To you, I was nothing more than a connection."

Kevin grabbed my hand. "It's time to go."

"That's what the music industry does to you Lorraine. It hurts people."

I kept my head down as I got into the car. I didn't want Kevin to see my tears.

"Is that why you came tonight because you knew?" I asked as he pulled off.

"I came because I wanted to protect you."

"I can't believe he did that."

"So, you'll give up this singing thing? You see now why I said it was dangerous?"

"Yes. Yes, I do."

He pulled over and leaned over to wipe the tears from my eyes. "I'm not trying to control you, Lorraine, despite what everyone else says or thinks. I love you. I know that's crazy. To be in love with someone after only a few days, but every time I'm with you, my heart beats harder than it's ever done before."

"Even more so than when you were with Semeerah?"

"Yes."

"Please don't lie to me, Kevin. I've had enough of that tonight. I want to know what's real."

"I'm real. What I feel for you is real. It's all-involving and abiding. For so long, I've had this fear of not being in control."

"Is it because of what happened? What happened to your mother?"

"Ms. M, told you?"

"She did."

"What else did she tell you?"

"She told me that because of that, that's why you might have been hurtful with Semeerah. Were you?"

He pulled away and leaned back in his seat. "Ms. M thinks every man is violent. She only sees what she wants to see. As I mentioned before, when I started working for Mrs. D, Semeerah was thirteen years old. I was Eighteen. I was just out of high school and living on the street. I was looking for a job. That's how I met Mrs. D, she was here to visit Semeerah and the manager of her boutique here, had just quit. It was good timing in a way for both of us.

"Ms. M was taking care of Semeerah while Mrs. D went back to Chicago. Her boutique there was also having its own share of problems and Semeerah's music career was really starting to take off. Semeerah and I had become close friends, and I admit that when she turned twenty-one, I thought it might have been possible, but then, I could see how much the music industry was changing her. So much that I didn't recognize her anymore.

"Earlier this year, right after she turned twenty-three, she flew home to Chicago to see Mrs. D and her father. She was supposed to have been on tour. Her and Mrs. D, got into a huge argument about something and Semeerah left and come back to New York. I picked her up and went we went back to Mrs. D's, apartment.

"We were sitting on the bed in Semeerah's room when she told me what she and Mrs. D had fought about. She was so hurt and angry, but it wasn't at me. I tried to get her to be reasonable, instead of going and doing something stupid.

"Over the years, whenever she and Mrs. D got into an agreement, Semeerah would go out and do something stupid. It became a dangerous trend. This time wasn't much different, and yet, it was different in so many ways.

"I could see it in Semeerah's eyes. The pain that was there. It was deep.

"She wouldn't listen to me. When she went to walk away, I reached out and grabbed her arm. It wasn't anything meant to hurt her in any way. By then, Ms. M was standing in the doorway. What Ms. M didn't see or hear, was when Semeerah asked me to let her go, I did so immediately.

"Anyway, about a month later, Mrs. D had come to New York to meet Semeerah there. She thought they could talk and try to work things out, but Semeerah being Semeerah, had run off and got married."

"So, you and Semeerah dated?"

"No. Never. We've never dated. Never kissed, never did anything. I swear to you. But I do care. Like I said, I love her, but not the way everyone keeps insisting. Do you believe me?"

I reached out and touched his cheek. "I do."

"I belong only to you Lorraine. I'm falling in love with you. Please believe me."

I placed my fingers on his lips. "Can I kiss you?"

FORTY

"I think I got everything just about ready." Ms. M stated, as she stood in the doorway of my bedroom.

"You frying chicken?"

"Of course. I seasoned it, and now it's sitting in the buttermilk, I'll have it ready by the time Semeerah walks in that door. Kevin still picking her up at three?"

"He is."

"Too bad Mrs. D ain't coming."

"I still would like to know what happened between the two of them," I said.

"Maybe Semeerah will tell ya."

"I'm sure she won't."

She glanced at her watch.

"You ain't going in today?"

"I'm going to get my hair done first, then, I'll go in for a few hours."

"You gonna be here for my fried chicken, right?"

"Of course. I should be back by the time Kevin arrives with Semeerah."

"It's mighty nice of ya to let him go get her. I don't think I would."

"Ms. M, let's not start this all over again."

"What? I'm just saying how nice you are, that's all."

"Sure you were, and I can fry chicken as good as you."

She laughed. "Good one."

I climbed out of bed.

"I better get showered so I can get out of here."

"I still can't believe she still married. I thought by now, that would be done and over."

"Ms. M."

"It's true, I did. Anyway, I hear he's coming in a couple of days."

"You never told me why she's coming?"

"She can't be coming just to see me?"

"Of course. I'm sure she can't wait to see you."

"You getting sassy with me, child?"

"No ma'am."

"Good, cause I'm still the adult up in here."

"I have to get going Ms. M."

"Well, I ain't stopping you. Get your shower, I got you some breakfast. It's on the counter."

"Why Ms. M that's mighty sweet of you to get up and fix me some breakfast." I winked at her.

"Whatever, child. I'll see you this afternoon."

She pulled something out of her apron.

"I almost done forgot. This here letter come for you the other day."

"A letter? From who?"

"It's from the guy you were with on the bus with. David, I think he said his name was. He came by the other day and left it for you."

"David was here?"

"He was. He came here two days ago. I was watching *Oprah*."

"And you are just now telling me."

"I ain't really seen you until this morning. You work all day, and then you and Kevin go out just about every night."

"We don't go out every night, and I was here with you watching television, two days ago."

She placed the letter on my bed. "Child, you and I both know that you were only here because Kevin had to change out the boutique's window display, two nights ago."

"True, but I was here. That's all I'm saying."

She glanced at the letter. "You gonna read it?"

"I don't know. Did you?"

"Of course I didn't. You know I ain't one to pry into other people's business."

"Of course, you would never do such a thing."

We both laughed.

"Kevin got some competition if you ask me. That David was mighty cute. He Spanish, but he cute."

"How do you know he's Spanish?"

"Child, you done forgot who you talking to."

"David isn't competition. I hope I never see him again and if he comes here again, I think we should call the police or something."

"Well, I don't' blame you, child. What that young man tried to do to you was an absolute shame, but it doesn't surprise me. That's how men are."

"Not all men, Ms. M."

"Child you young, so you would say that. However, I still think he was mighty cute."

"Bye Ms. M."

She turned and walked out of my room.

My hands shook as I picked it up. I glanced at the doorway to see if Ms. M, had gone.

"Go ahead and read it, child. You know you want to. Forgiveness ain't never hurt anyone."

I opened it.

Dear Lorraine,

I'm sorry.

I know those words seem meaningless. I know what I did took away their worth, but I believe you know that I really did it for him. For Jeffery.

I can't apologize for my motives, but I do apologize for the way that I went about carrying them out.

Here is the truth.

On the bus to Atlanta, I had listened carefully to the conversation you and Mrs. D had. I had heard just about every word, and I saw it as my chance.

I saw you as my connection.

I got the gig at the Skinny because I told Misty that I had someone that could be even bigger than Semeerah. I told her about you and how you had a real voice. A voice with depth and meaning. I told her that the world would love you because they wouldn't believe that a voice like that, one with soul, could come out of a white girl. I told her that you only looked white, but that you were really black. I explained how we could use that to reach both the white and black audience.

I told her that if she gave you a shot, I would bring you in on Friday to perform. She finally agreed, but only after I told her about how Mrs. Dena Fox had been on the bus, and how she was going to introduce you to her daughter, and that her daughter was putting together her own record label.

It wasn't hard for me to figure out who Mrs. D's daughter was.

I pitched you hard Lorraine, using fear. Fear that Semeerah would get to you first, if Misty didn't act. That's how I got her.

Now, I just need you.

I want to be your Manager.

Misty is ready to sign you on, but only if you seriously want a career in music. She can deliver that Lorraine. I have negotiated a great record deal for you. One that many new artists never see until they've been in the industry for years and have proved their worth.

That's what I bring to the table. Here is what I leave off of it... no more games. No more dishonesty.

Please, Lorraine, let me be your manager.

We both know that computers are not right for you. Don't give up your passion.

I bet he's going after his dreams. Yes, I'm speaking about Kevin. Is it fair to ask you to put aside your own dreams, before you've even had a chance to discover the possibilities that your dreams could lead to?

Give me another chance. Better yet, give your dreams a chance.

If not for yourself, for her. Ella.

I am and will always be your friend,

David.

I sat on the bed and re-read the letter three times before I placed it on my nightstand.

FORTY-ONE

She was sitting on the sofa as I walked into the apartment. No wig, like the ones she often wore for her cover albums. No make-up. Just a smile, a simple shirt and a pair of blue jeans.

"Wow, they weren't kidding. You really are the white version of me." She said, as she quickly walked over to me and wrapped her arms around me. "It's so good to finally meet you, Lorraine. Mrs. D, kept urging me to get back to New York to hear you, although Kevin here, seems to be against it." She shot Kevin a quick glance.

"Mrs. D? Don't you mean your mother?"

She ignored my question. "So, how long have you been singing?"

"I guess for a while. It's never been anything professional. Is that why you're here, to hear me sing?"

"Of course. I would have come sooner, but with the funeral, interviews, and life, I'm just able to make it. Plus, with the baby and all, on the way."

"You're pregnant?" I asked as I glanced to see Kevin's reaction.

He had none. I was relieved. Ms. M's facial expression was another matter of course.

"Not yet, but we're working on it." She placed her hands on her stomach. "So Kevin tells me that you sang at The Skinny, for Misty. Is that right?"

"Well, it wasn't really for her."

She stared at me. "So, you ready?"

"Ma'am?"

"Girl please, no one calls me Ma'am. Besides, we're the same age. Ma'am is for Mrs. D."

She sat back down. "I was asking if you were ready to sing for me? I'm sorry, I don't mean to rush, but I've got to get to my hotel. I came straight here, but I've got an early morning and Daniel, my husband is coming in very soon as well." She glanced at Kevin again as she twirled her ring finger around.

"Semeerah, I told you in the car that Lorraine isn't interested in singing."

"I'm ready." I glared at Kevin.

He glared back, but, I didn't back down.

"Good." She looked at Kevin. "I see you're still the same old Kevin."

"I'm not trying to control anything Semeerah."

"Sure you are. It's what you do. Lorraine, please, go ahead."

I placed my purse on the table and took a few steps back. I knew I should have been nervous, but I wasn't.

Ms. M leaned up against the wall.

"Do you need me to count you in?"

"What's that?"

She laughed. "Never mind, just start whenever you're ready."

I closed my eyes and allowed my dreams to rule me. I could feel them rushing through me. Taking over everything that I was and wanted to be. It was a good feeling. A natural one.

I heard Ms. M clapping as I opened my eyes. "Child, you got a voice on ya. I wouldn't have believed it, but, I heard it myself."

Kevin got up and walked away.

"Kevin."

"Let him go. He'll get over it. Mrs. D was right to keep after me. She even spoke of you at the funeral. That woman knows she got an eye for talent."

"Why do you call her that, Mrs. D? Isn't she your mother?"

"I thought so for twenty-three years."

"Semeerah!"

"What, Ms. M, you know it's true! She lied to me."

"That might be true, but now is not the time or the place, child."

"She might as well know. She might as well know that the great Mrs. D is nothing but a liar!"

"She's the only mother you got Semeerah. She loves you. Stop this foolishness child. Stop it right now. You hear me? I ain't going to stand for it no more. You know she'd give the world and everything in it for you. You've got to forgive her Semeerah. You've got to move on."

"Why? Why do I have to forgive her?"

"Because she's your mother. That's why."

"How can I Ms. M? How can I? She should have told me the truth. All this time and she never told me, never told me that I was....that I was adopted."

"Semeerah Fox!"

"Stop calling me that. It's not my name! We don't really know what my real last name is, do we Ms. M!"

Kevin walked back in. "I'm taking you to your hotel Semeerah."

"Stop trying to boss me around. I'm not one of the kids from the shop, I keep trying to tell you that."

"Semeerah, stop it. I mean it child. Don't be nasty."

"Oh yes, I forgot...I am. I'm no different than them. Mrs. D had to save me too. Isn't that right Kevin?"

"Let's go Semeerah."

"I'll take a cab."

"No, you won't. You know the press or someone will recognize you." He went to reach for her, but she pulled away.

"Yes, I will!"

"Semeerah, let Kevin take you to your hotel. Ain't no need in taking a cab and causing a scene."

"I'm not a child anymore Ms. M! I'm a grown, married woman who makes more money than you've seen in your lifetime. If I want to take a cab, I will."

"You might be married, but you apparently ain't grown up enough. Now grab your suitcase and get your behind in the car with Kevin. I mean what I say Semeerah!"

She grabbed her purse and walked toward the door. "Fine! Are you coming, Kevin?"

I watched as he walked toward the door. I could see the sadness in his eyes. "I'll be back in a few Lorraine, okay?"

All I could do was nod my head.

Ms. M sat down on the sofa and stared at the ceiling for a moment after they left. "I'm sorry child. You shouldn't have witnessed all of that. Semeerah's heart is still hurting from finding out the truth, that's all. She didn't mean to be rude."

"Now I guess I know what happened between her and Mrs. D."

"I feel for both of them. Mrs. D, I guess, should have told that child a long time ago that she was adopted."

"How did Semeerah find out?"

"She overheard Mrs. D and that no-good husband of hers. They got into a fight, and he blurted it out. Between the two of us, I think he did it on purpose. Poor child. She didn't take it too well. I can't say I blame her, but, it's time that she forgives Mrs. D, and remembers all the good Mrs. D done did for her."

"I know how she felt Ms. M. It wasn't long ago that I found out that I was adopted. My father told me. Actually, when I met Mrs. D, I was on my way to try and find my birth mother or at least her family. Mrs. D promised me that if I came to New York, she would look for her for me, but I haven't heard from Mrs. D, since."

"Well, I'm sure Mrs. D will keep her promise, child. I ain't ever known her not to, but you got to give her time. She got her own heart that needs to heal."

"I understand."

"I know you do. You got more sense and kindness than Semeerrah, that's for sure. Shoot, we all think our problems is king until we see someone else got their pieces of life moving across the board. If you ask me, we all running away from check-mate child."

"One day Ms. M, you aren't going to have a saying for everything."

"That's true, but that time ain't come yet, child."

"My birth mother is black." I blurted out.

"Well, that explains the voice."

"There are plenty of white folks that can sing Ms. M."

"Yes, but it ain't many that got soul in the depth of their voice like you do. That is inherited. You can blow child. I mean, I was impressed, and I don't get impressed by much. I'm sure when Semeerah calms her behind down, she'll call you."

"Do you think she really thought I could sing?"

"You know it doesn't really matter what she thought. Do you believe you can sing?"

"I guess."

"You know what they say about guessing?"

"No, what do they say about it?"

"They say that it ain't worth more than a hill of beans. Shoot, I guess it gonna rain tomorrow, that don't mean I believe that it will."

"You read the letter from David, didn't you?"

"I ain't saying if I did or if I didn't."

"You think I should sing, don't you? I don't think I realized it before, but I love to sing. I also love..."

"Kevin. Child, anybody can see that. It seems to be that you got two roads in front of you. They both be filled with pebbles and stones. Ain't no way in life ever smooth, but only you can determine which one you willing to put your feet on. He will come with you, no matter which road you take. It will take him some time. I was wrong about him. I see that now."

"You know what I think Ms. M? I believe you read my letter."

"Like I said, maybe I did and maybe I didn't."

I watched as she walked out of my room.

"Go ahead and read it again. It ain't gonna hurt."

I headed toward my room.

FORTY-TWO

Just as I went to pull David's letter out, my phone rang.

"Lorraine, is that you?"

I thought my heart was going to stop. "Daddy?" I sat down on the edge of my bed.

"Yes, it's me."

"How? How did you get this number?"

"Some guy named Kevin left a message on the voicemail."

"Kevin called you?"

"He did. How are you?"

"I'm alright daddy. When did Kevin call you?"

"About two weeks ago, but I just found out."

"Why is that?"

"You know the answer to that."

"I know I'm not supposed to hate anyone Daddy, but I hate that woman. I wish you had never married her."

"Why did you leave Lorraine? When I got back to the house that day, you were gone."

"You should ask Old Big Bones."

"Who?"

"Your wife. Ella and I use to call her Old Big Bones."

"I see. I did ask her."

"What did she tell you?"

"She said that you left because of what I told you. What I told you about your birth mother. She also said that you were headed to find her."

"Some of that is true."

"I wish you had of waited until I got back. Clarissa was the one that told you that you were..."

"Black? Yes, she was the one that told me."

"I'm so sorry Lorraine. I really am. I messed up so much. I didn't realize how much of a problem my drinking had really become. I should have never allowed her to do the things that she did. She's gone now."

"She left you?"

"No, I put her out. I'm divorcing her."

"Daddy, how is Ella. Can I speak to her? Does she hate me?"

He grew quiet. "Ella isn't here. That's why I'm calling."

"Where is she?"

"I don't know how to tell you this Lorraine."

"Tell me what? What is it? Is Ella hurt?"

"Ella ran away."

"What do you mean she ran away? When?" I stood up.

"She left a couple of days after you did. She told Clarissa that she was going to find you. That she was going to Atlanta."

"What! She's fourteen years old!"

"I know how old she is Lorraine."

"Did you call the police? Did you report her missing?"

"Of course I did. We've been looking for her ever since. Every single day."

"Are you drunk Daddy? Have you still been drinking?"

"Don't raise your voice Lorraine, and no I haven't been drinking. I haven't had a drink since you left that day."

"I'm sorry, I just can't believe this." I sat back down and balled my comforter up in my hands to keep me calm. "Do you think she made it to Atlanta? Did she have any money? Did she have any food? Oh, Daddy, I can't believe this. I knew I shouldn't have left. She was my responsibility. I promised her that I would always protect her. I promised daddy."

"She did make it there. She's in Atlanta. She made it to Barrow County, and it was never your responsibility Lorraine. It was mine. I've got a lot of making up to do. To both of you."

"How do you know she made it there? Did she call?"

"I got a call from the police there. They found her."

"When? When did they find her?"

"I got the call this morning."

"And you're just now calling me?"

"Like I said, I didn't know where you were. I only got a chance to listen to Kevin's message a few minutes ago. Anyway, the Barrow County police assured me that she will be okay."

"What do you mean? Did she get hurt?"

"There was an accident. It seems she slipped on some rocks in a river there and she was found unconscious. They thought she was dead."

I screamed.

"Lorraine, I'm heading down there now. I've been trying to get a flight. I just got the tickets."

I hung up.

"Ms. M!"

She had come running in my room.

"Call Mrs. D, I need a plane ticket to Atlanta."

"What is it, child?"

Kevin walked in my room.

"What's going on?"

"It's my sister. They found her in Atlanta. There was some sort of accident. She almost died. I need to get there right now!"

"I'll get us plane tickets. Ms. M, help her pack please."

"Why didn't you tell me?"

"Tell you what?"

"That you called my father."

"Mrs. D asked me to call him and let him know where you were. She figured he would be worried. I called several times and never got anyone on the phone. I left a voicemail. Honestly, I thought he would have called before now."

"My step-mother, that wicked woman didn't give him the message. He only found out about it today. This is all my fault. I should never have left her."

"We will get there as fast as we can Lorraine."

"This is like a nightmare."

He wrapped me in arms as I sobbed.

"Thank you, Kevin. Thank you."

"You don't have to thank me, Lorraine. I love you."

My phone rang again.

"Lorraine, it's me, David."

"David, I don't have time to talk."

I slammed the phone down.

"Was that your father again?"

"No, it was David. Can we go? Can we leave now! I don't need a suitcase, I just need to get there."

"I understand. Ms. M, call Mrs. D, tell her what's going on. Tell her that I'll call her as soon as we get there. Call the store and let them know I'm not coming back today."

"You want her to get the tickets?"

"I'll purchase them when we get to the airport."

FORTY-THREE

Honour Blue Baker

I felt the touch of the sun as I opened my eyes. I immediately jumped up and stared at my mother. I thought I saw her hand move.
I watched it carefully.

Ten minutes later, I was still watching her when Aaron walked into the room holding two cups of coffee and a bag that was hanging off his arm.

"Anything change?"

"No." I grabbed a cup and watched as he sat down.

He glanced at the cot.

"You were right, it wasn't very comfortable," I said.

"Honestly, I'm just glad to see it was used. I was worried that maybe you ran off during the night with Bryan."

I just looked at him.

"Have the doctors been in yet?"

"No, her doctor hasn't come in yet."

"But Bryan I take it has?"

"I just got up, Aaron."

"He was here last night, though."

"Can we not do this?" I glanced at my mother.

"I'm sorry. You're right, now is not the time. I brought you a change of clothes and a few other things I saw in your room that you might need."

"Thanks. They let you into my room."

"They did once I told them I was your Fiancé."

"Aaron."

"What? You needed clothes, didn't you?"

"I do. Thank you, but please stop telling people that."

He grew quiet.

"What is it?" I asked.

"I have something else to tell you."

"What?"

"Your attorney called my office after he couldn't get a hold of you. You've been cleared. It looks like you can open your salon back up again."

"I'm surprised he said he couldn't reach me, I've had my phone on." I got up and went to my purse. I pulled my cell phone out and noticed that it had gone dead.

"Will you open the salon back up?"

"I don't know."

"Can you?"

I sat back down.

"I don't know. I haven't had much time to really think about it. I suppose it would be hard for me to walk back in there. There so much pain behind those walls now. I've been thinking about opening one up here."

He stared at me. I knew what he wanted to ask, but he didn't.

"I wish I could go back and undo all the pain I caused you Honour. I really do."

"So do I, but you can't."

"No, I can't."

I stood up. Aaron watched me move towards the window. "This all sounds like a broken record. Like some blues song in the making."

"Do you want to forgive me Honour?"

I turned toward him, leaning on the window ledge. "My mama

always taught me that forgiveness was freedom. So yes, I want to forgive you and one day I shall. But today is not that day Aaron. You can't expect it to be."

He came and stood in front of me.

"I lost you didn't I Honour?"

I grabbed his hands and held them in mine. "Yes."

There were tears in both of our eyes.

He placed a kiss on my cheek and started toward the door.

"Aaron, wait, let me give you your..."

"You keep it, Honour. I told you that it belonged to you."

FORTY-FOUR

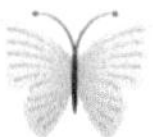

The doctor examined mama. There was no change.

Just before he left, he told me to keep talking to her, that sometimes hearing the voice of a loved one helps.

I placed her hand on mine as I sat by her bed.

"Do you think I did the right thing Mama? I know you heard us. Was I a fool to let him go? He hurt me, Mama." I paused and glanced toward the window. "But he wasn't the first man to do so Mama. The first man was Paul King." The tears streaked down my cheeks as I tried to get it out. "I know you liked him, Mama. I know you thought the world of him, but he took my world from me. He did Mama. He raped me.

"You remember that day Mama, that day that you sent me over to drop off your Peach Cobbler because Mrs. King, his wife, was sick and you wanted to give her something to cheer her up?

"I did what you had asked me. I went there. I knocked on the door, only Mrs. King wasn't home. She had gone to the doctor. Mr. King came to the door, and he told me to come on in and put the Cobbler on the table in the kitchen. So I did. I went inside the house, and I placed your Cobbler on the table, just like he told me to.

"I was getting ready to leave when he said that he had some peppermint upstairs. He said it was in their bedroom on the dresser. I knew how much you liked his peppermint Mama, so I went up to get it.

"When I got up there, I didn't see it. So, I leaned over the balcony and told Mr. King that I didn't see it. It wasn't any peppermint on the dresser Mama. I swear it wasn't. Mr. King told me to just hold on, and he'd come up. He said that Mrs. King must have moved it somewhere and he'd come up and find it for me.

"That's what he did. He came into their bedroom and started looking around it like he was looking for the peppermint. I stood against the dresser waiting for him to find it so I could leave.

"He came over to the dresser and starting moving stuff and looking under stuff. I told him that I could just come back when he found it, but he told me just to wait, he was sure it was just somewhere he was overlooking. He told me to go look on the side of their bed. By the nightstand. I did. That's when he came over and grabbed me.

"He hit me so hard Mama. He tore my dress, but I fought him, Mama. Remember that blue dress you made for me? The one I used to wear so much, you had to let out the hem to make it longer, as I got older. The one that daddy loved. That's the dress Mama. That's the dress that holds all my shame.

"I want you to know Mama, I want you to know that I screamed for you. I cried for daddy, but no one was there to save me. No one Mama. It's was just me.

"I remember when I got home. You were angry with me. Angry that I had torn my dress. Why couldn't you see the pain I was in Mama? Why didn't you look hard enough? I told you that I had fallen and that's how I had torn it. I told you that because when I looked at your face Mama, I knew. I knew you wouldn't believe me.

"You and I never seem to see each other as mother and daughter after that. But I love you, Mama. I really love you. It took me a long time to see that I couldn't blame you. I could only blame him.

"There's something else Mama. Something else that I have to tell you. I've been keeping it locked up inside me for so many years Mama. So many dark years.

"I could feel it eating away at me. But, I don't want to carry the past anymore in the pit of my kidneys Mama. I want to breathe. I want peace.

"When I went away to college. I was pregnant. Four months actually. I had to wait a semester to start school because of it. That's why I didn't graduate when you thought I should have. It wasn't because I had been goofing off Mama. It was because I had to wait.

"The day I was about to give birth, I met this wonderful woman and her husband. They were a young white couple that had been trying to have children. She had just suffered a fourth miscarriage, and because of her cancer, they had decided to adopt.

"They had the adoption agency come to the hospital the next day after I had given birth. Mama, I gave birth to two girls. Two girls, Mama. One came out white as Mr. King Mama. The other had my skin tone. But they both were beautiful, Mama. I held them in my arms, and I cried with them, Mama. I cried all night. I almost couldn't do it, Mama. I almost couldn't give them up.

"I wish you could have seen them, Mama. I wish they could have known how much I loved them.

"The young white couple Mama, they came, and they adopted the one girl I named Lorraine. I named her after your sister, Mama.

"The other one, I gave your mama's first name, Semeerah.

"Semeerah was adopted by a woman that I never got a chance to meet. I don't even know her name or how she looks, but the agency assured me that she would take good care of Semeerah.

"They should be around twenty-three-years-old now. There's not a day that goes by when I don't think of them, Mama. Not a day. I tell myself that they both have had a wonderful life. One filled with love. I tell myself this Mama to ease the pain. To ease the pain of not seeing them. Not holding them. Not being with them.

"I'd give anything Mama to see them today, as they are now. To hear them speak. To look in their eyes and see some part of me. I couldn't do so back them, Mama. I just couldn't. When I saw them back then, all I saw was his face in their eyes.

"No mother should look at their own children like that and knew I couldn't put them through the kind of tragedy. It wouldn't have been fair.

"Tell me I did the right thing Mama."

I grabbed her hand and wiped my skin with it. A mother's touch. It was still strong. I still longed for it. Needed it.

I heard someone move. When I turned around, I saw Bryan standing there.

FORTY-FIVE

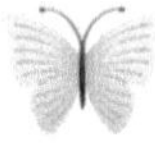

"Bryan, I didn't hear you come in."

"I'm sorry, I should have said something."

I began trying to wipe the tears away. "How long, how long have you been standing there?"

He came and knelt down beside me. "Long enough."

"You heard?"

"I heard."

"Oh, Bryan."

He grabbed me and held me in his arms, where I cried.

"It helps, doesn't it? To let go. To talk about the things that try to make us unrepairable."

"It does." I took a deep breath and glanced at my mother. "I only wish she were awake. I don't know if I could do it again."

"I know I said that I wouldn't do this...but when Stephanie and I got divorced, she was pregnant by him. You asked if she and I had kids and I told you that she never wanted any. The truth is, she just never wanted any with me. I can't tell you what something like that does to a man. I'm not comparing it to what happened to you, but, it took me a long time to find my peace."

"How did you do it?"

"I found someone I could talk to. I joined a support group. It was a support group for divorced men. I found that I could tell the members of that group, things that I dared not say to anyone else because I felt like no one else could have possibly understood what I went through. How I felt. That group helped me Honour. They helped me find my peace and helped me feel as if I could love again."

"So, you think I should join a support group?"

"I can't tell you what to do, but, I can ask you to give it consider ation. It's a sad thing, but there are many women and men, who have gone through what you did."

"I'll think about it. I'm not making any promises, but I will think about it."

He stood up.

"Bryan, I didn't share this with her doctor, but, when I woke up this morning, I could have sworn I saw her hand move. Have the test come back yet?"

"They haven't." He walked over and examined her.

"What if she doesn't wake up? How long can she be in a coma before something even more serious occurs, like brain damage?"

"A coma can last for two to four weeks. There are cases where patients have been in a coma for years. When she wakes up, if she needs anything like Physiotherapy, I will make sure she gets the very best care."

I reached for my mother's hand again. "Do you think there is any chance she heard me? The doctor told me to talk to her, although I'm sure he didn't have that 'kind' of talking in mind."

He placed his hand on my shoulders. "We always encourage loved one to talk to comatose patients like they would if they were awake. We even suggest being careful what is said, because there is that possibility of being heard." He looked down at my mother. "You know growing up, your mother always heard everything, so I wouldn't be surprised, if when she wakes up, she wants to know if you married Aaron or me."

"Why? Aaron is the only one who proposed."

"That's right, so I guess I had better get down on my knee and throw my ring in the mix."

Before I could get a word out, he was down on one knee.

"Honour Blue Baker, my love for you is true. It does not come to you with the strings of the past attached as if it needs the past to survive. It comes to you breathing, thirsting, and beating for the future. I knew the moment I laid eyes on you again that I could never love anyone else as deeply and as passionately, as I love you. My love for you is immutable. You will never have to question if it will last. Even if you should say no. Even if you should choose Aaron, you have to know that my heart, my soul, all that I am, belongs to you. I leave nothing out.

"Honour Blue Baker, I love you. Be my wife."

I pulled him to me and wrapped my arms around his waist. I stroked the side of his cheek and allowed my fingers to connect with the outline of his jawline. I stared into his eyes and allowed my lungs to be exposed. The part of me that was breathing in the weight of his feelings.

My lips parted, and the words that would bridge our past with our future slipped off of them.

"Bryan, for so long I had denied my past, but I had forgotten that not everything in it was ugly. Not everything that touched me lacked tenderness. I had forgotten that there was you. You were always there. You are my sun after the storm, and I want to dance in the rain of your love forever. My answer is yes." I placed my lips upon him, and that's when I felt it.

A wave of peace.

It spread through my body like a flower that was feeling the touch of spring, for the very first time.

The box was not velvet. But it was perfect.

Perfect in every way that mattered.

FORTY-SIX

We could hear his name being paged over the intercom.

"I don't want to leave you, but I have to make my rounds."

"Go. I understand."

He kissed me again and headed toward the door. "Thank you."

I glanced down at my hand. My eyes resting for a second on my ring finger. My smile filled my entire body. From the tip of my toes to each strand of hair on my head.

I was still smiling when the nurse came in.

"Good morning, Ms. Baker."

"Good morning, Rosa. Do you think you could stay with her until I get showered and changed?"

"No problem, ma'am."

"Thank you so much. I promised to be quick. I'm going to use the one in mama's bathroom here."

"Take your time, Ms. Emma is the last patient on my rounds this morning."

"Perfect."

I watched as Rosa sat down on the side of mama's bed before I ran into the bathroom.

About fifteen minutes later, as I was standing in front of the mirror, I thought I heard Rosa calling me.

"Ms. Baker, is this your mama's..."

I stuck my head out of the bathroom. Rosa was getting up off the floor on the side of mama's bed. "Everything okay?" I asked.

She smiled. "Oh yes, ma'am. I was just picking up something that I dropped that's all. Do you mind if I turn on the television station?"

"Sure." I watched her grab the remote and click on the TV.

I ducked back into the bathroom to finish brushing my teeth.

When I finally stepped back out, I looked up and saw Jimmy. "What happened Rosa?"

"They have been interviewing him about that girl Ms. Emma found in the river. It's big news. Be on all morning. Sheriff Jimmy said that the girl is from Chicago."

"So, he finally asked her where she was from?"

"Looks like it. I heard that the family has been looking for her for over two weeks."

"Wow. I wonder why in the world she came all the way to Atlanta from Chicago, and by herself, for that matter."

"It seems she was looking for her sister."

Bryan, walked back into the room. "Turn the television up some, Nurse Rosa. I think you should hear this Honour."

Rosa, grabbed the remote again and adjusted the volume.

We all stood with our eyes glued to the screen. I couldn't believe what I was hearing.

"Sheriff Jimmy, what can you tell us about the King's involvement? Is the young girl found by Mrs. Emma Lee Baker, related to them?"

Jimmy tilted his hat so that the camera could get a good shot of him. "Not that we can gather. We do know that she had their address. It appears her older sister may have been more connected to them, than her, but we can't confirm or deny that, at this time."

"So it has been confirmed that the young girl came here to Barrow County looking for her older sister?"

"Yes. I interviewed the young girl myself, and I can confirm that she came her looking for her older sister. Of course, because of the young girl's age, we can't release her name."

"Can you tell us the name of her older sister? Is she living here in Barrow County? What do you know about her?"

"We know that the older sister was adopted and that the birth mother might have lived here at some point. From what we can gather, the older sister, however, has never lived in Barrow County, but, we do know that she is on her way here."

"Is that why the young girl thought her older sister was here in Barrow County because the birth mother might have lived here at some point?"

"It is."

"Can you tell us the name of the birth mother?"

"We can't release that information at this time."

"Can you tell us when the birth mother might have lived here?"

"We can't release that information at this time."

"But that information is in your possession?"

"We can't say at this time."

"Can't or won't?"

"Same thing in my book."

"Perhaps not for the residents of Barrow County. I'm sure they would like to know."

"If we deem it necessary, we will release that information. As of right now, I can't discuss it."

"So you speak for the whole police department?"

"I am the Sheriff, ain't I?"

"You are. Are we correct to assume then, that there has been some contact with the young girl's family?"

Jimmy adjusted his hat again. "There has been telephone contact with the father. Once this morning, and then again, a few hours ago. He and the older sister are due to arrive shortly."

"Can you tell us about the alleged allegations against Mr. King. Is it true that he might have committed a crime that connects him to the birth mother? If so, can you tell us about that?"

"Well, seeing that the Kings have long done passed, we can't be too sure about those alleged allegations, but there will be an investigation into the matter."

"So, you can't confirm that Mr. King might have sexually assaulted

the birth mother, years ago? We have reliable sources that suggest that this was the case, can you confirm or deny that?"

"As I stated, we will be conducting a full investigation, until that time, I can't confirm or deny that."

"But, it might be possible?"

Jimmy, shifted his feet some. "Well now, anything is possible, but until we get the facts, it will stay at that."

"Will you be interviewing the older sister's birth mother?"

"The details of how we will proceed with our investigation can't be shared with the public at this time. Mr. King and his family were respected members of this community and therefore are innocent until proven guilty."

"So you do know who the birth mother is?"

"You've asked that already."

"Can you tell us about the locket?"

"How do you know about that?"

"Like I said, we have our reliable sources. What can you tell us about the locket? We've been told that it somehow confirms who the birth mother is. That there's a picture of the birth mother inside of it. Do you have the locket?"

"We do not have the gold locket in our possession, at this time. We are still looking for it."

"So, the locket does exist, and it's gold, is that correct?"

Jimmy, glared at the reporter.

"We can't deny or confirm the existence of the locket since we haven't seen it or been able to recover it."

"Do you think the community will still respect Mr. King if your investigation shows that he is indeed guilty of these alleged allegations?"

"I reckon not, but I can't speak for the community, now can I?"

"Will you, if Mr. King is found guilty of these alleged allegations?"

"I respect the law and have an obligation to it."

"Can you tell us how much money Mr. King contributed to your police department over the years."

The camera zoomed in on Jimmy's face.

"That information has nothing to do with this case."

"Our research tells us that Mr. King was accused of sexual assault

while he resided in New York, but because of a technicality, the case had to be dismissed? Can you confirm this?"

"We can't. This is Barrow County, not New York. But we will be contacting them."

"What about the fact that he was disbarred as an Attorney, can you confirm that?"

"We can't."

"Sheriff Jimmy, one last question."

"Go ahead."

"How would it look if your police department allowed a rapist to reside for over thirty years in a family community like Barrow County? Wasn't your father the Sheriff when the Kings arrived?"

"Get that microphone out of my face! This interview is over!"

FORTY-SEVEN

"Rosa, do you think you could give us a moment."

"Sure thing Doctor. Let me just fix Ms. Emma's pillow first."

"Thank you."

Bryan and I turned back to the television.

"There. I'll just head back to the Nurse's station. Call me Ms. Baker, if you need me for anything. I still can't believe your mama was the one to find that young girl. Her name is Ella by the way. Sheriff Jimmy can't say, but I can. She's a cute little thing. She's terribly smart. Despite what he says, she talks."

"Thank you, Nurse Rosa. Ms. Baker will call the nurse's station if she needs anything."

"Yes, Doctor."

I could hear Rosa open and close the door, but my eyes remained on the television. My heart was beating so hard and so fast, I thought I would lose my balance.

"Honour, why don't you sit down."

I couldn't. I couldn't get my body to move. I felt like I was glued to the floor. Like my eyes were glued to the television. All I wanted to do was run. Run back to Chicago.

"Honour."

"Can you give me a moment by myself Bryan?"

"Honour, you don't have to face this alone."

I turned and stared at him.

"Did you tell them? Did you say who I am?"

"No. Why would you think I did? Do you really think I would do such a thing?"

"I could see it on Jimmy's face. He knows I'm the birth mother. He knows what Paul did to me. Did you tell them?"

"I told you I didn't. Did it occur to you that maybe the young girl knew your name? Did you consider that before accusing me?"

I turned and stared at the television again. The tears streamed down my face.

My peace had packed its bag and left.

"Can you just give me a moment, can you leave?"

"Honour."

"Leave!"

"No. I'm not leaving you. Years ago I saw you come out of that house. I tried to be there for you, but you pushed me away, and I let you. I won't do that again. I love you Honour. You hear me? I love you. I will not be pushed away again. We will face this together. Always together, Honour, okay?"

I nodded as he placed his arms around me.

"She's coming here, Bryan."

"She is, that's a fact we can't change now."

"What am I going to do?"

"You're going to have to face her. I'll be there with you. Right by your side."

"She will hate me."

"Yes, she will. At first. But in time, that might change."

"What if it doesn't?"

"We can't stand in a world of "what if's" Honour. No one can."

I stared at my mother. "The locket."

"Where is it?"

I searched around her bed. I couldn't find it anywhere. Then I looked at my mama's chest."

"You don't think she put it in there, do you?"

"She put everything in there."

"Well, you're her daughter."

"You're a doctor."

He stepped back.

"Daughters first."

I patted the outside of my mama's hospital gown. "I don't feel anything."

"You're going to have to look Honour. You're her daughter, I'm sure you've seen them before."

"Yeah, when I was a newborn."

"Nothing like going back in the past." He laughed.

"You got jokes." I carefully placed my hand under my mama's gown and closed my eyes, and I tried to feel for the locket.

"You don't feel it?"

I pulled away. "No, I don't, and I pray to never have to do that again. My mother would slap me if she were awake."

"She would."

"Thanks."

"Look around her pillow."

I lifted up her pillow and pulled the locket out.

We both stared at it.

"You know you're going to have to turn that over to Sheriff Jimmy?"

"Why?"

"You sound like your mother?"

"I do, don't I? I'll give it to him." I turned the locket on its side. "It looks like it needs a key to open."

"Maybe the young girl has the key. She apparently told someone about the locket.

"You're right. I wonder if she will talk to me?" I headed toward the door.

"Where are you going?"

"What room is she in?"

"You can't go in her room, Honour."

"I have to. I need to talk to her. Please, Bryan, what room is she in."

"She's on the fifth floor. Room 5B."

"Thank you."

"Don't tell anyone I gave you that information."

"I won't. I'll blame Nurse Rosa."

"What? Why?"

"Mama didn't like her anyway, and I have a feeling she was the 'reliable source' the reporter spoke about."

He laughed. "Rosa probably was, come to think about it."

"Bryan, I'm sorry for accusing you."

"It's okay."

"It's not, but, I really am sorry. You still want to marry me."

"What, and miss out on our honeymoon! We've got twenty something years of making up to do."

"Bryan!"

"What? I'm just saying."

"I love you, Bryan, I really do."

"I'll need to hear that often on our honeymoon as well, now go."

FORTY-EIGHT
Lorraine

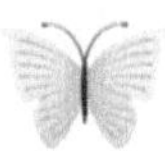

"I hung up on my father."

"He'll understand."

"I'm so scared Kevin."

"Didn't you say that your father told you that Ella will make a full recovery?"

"Yes, but, it's all my fault. If I hadn't left her."

"You didn't know this was going to happen Lorraine. It's not your fault. We'll be at the hospital in a few minutes so you can see that she's okay for yourself."

"You think my father is there already?"

"I don't know. He should be, but I don't know what time he was able to get a flight out for. Thank goodness for Mrs. D's connections at the airport, we might not have gotten a flight out ourselves so quickly."

"I just want to see her."

"You will. We're here."

I searched the hospital parking lot.

"Who are you looking for?"

"My father."

"He's probably already inside, come on."

We rushed inside and was directed to the 5th floor.

"My I help you?"

"I'm here to see my sister, Ella Chambers."

"You must be Lorraine. I've heard so much about you."

"Excuse me."

"I'm Rosa. I've been your sister's nurse."

"Is she alright?"

"She's doing just fine. She took a bump to the head, but she's recovered nicely. Your father is here. He arrived about ten minutes ago. Ella looks just like him. Come on, I'll take you to her room."

"I can't wait to see her."

"I know she feels the same. She hasn't talked about much else, except you. She and I been talking every day since she arrived. Good thing Ms. Emma found her when she did. Ella is such a sweet girl."

"She always has been."

"Here we are. This is her room. Her doctor will be in shortly. He's been a little tied up. You know how it is for doctors. Always busy." She smiled as she opened Ella's room door. "Ella, look who I found."

I couldn't contain my tears.

"Sister!" Ella shouted the moment she saw me.

I held her in my arms so tight and placed a few kisses on her forehead.

"Sister, I can't believe it's you."

"Ella, what were you thinking?"

"Hello, Lorraine?"

I let Ella go gently and looked up. "Daddy."

He got up from his chair and wrapped his arms around me.

"You don't know how happy I am to see you. To see both of my daughters. I love you both." He began to cry.

"It's okay, daddy."

"No, it's not good. If I had of been a father, none of this would have happened."

"I'm just happy we're all okay."

He held me tight. "I'm am too Lorraine. I promise I will make it up to you both. You will never have to worry about Clarissa again. I'm so sorry Lorraine. I'm so sorry Ella."

"I won't lie and say I'm not happy to hear that Ole Big Bones is gone."

We all laughed.

My father, looked up toward Kevin.

"You must be the young man that called?"

"Yes Sir, I am."

He let me go and grabbed Kevin. "Thank you. Thank you so much."

"Daddy, don't squeeze him to death."

He let Kevin go. "I'm sorry. I'm just so happy. I was beginning to wonder if this day would ever happen. To hold both of my girls again. Thank you."

Kevin, looked my way and smiled.

"We're still waiting for the doctor to come in, but, Ella looks great to me. I can't wait to take her home."

"She does." I hugged her again.

"I can't wait to take both of you home."

Kevin, glanced at me. I could see the fear on his face.

I walked over and grabbed his hand.

"Daddy, I'm not coming back to Chicago. I'm staying here."

"Lorraine here has a music deal waiting for her. She's going to sing."

I stared at him.

"Sister! I told you that you could sing. You're going to be famous!"

"Let's not get too excited."

"Lorraine, is that want you really want? To stay here and sing instead of coming home?"

I let go of Kevin's hand and sat down on the edge of the bed. "I want to stay here daddy. New York is my home now, but not because I have a music contract waiting for me." I glanced at Kevin. "I have a great job at a beautiful boutique. I enjoy it more than I thought I would and I don't think the music industry is right for me."

"Are you sure Lorraine? If you really want to sing, I will support you. I promise."

"I'm sure Kevin. It's my decision. One that I realized only I could make. I'm doing it for me."

He came over to me.

"But, I know that singing is really your passion. I know about the letter. The one David wrote to you."

"Who is David?"

I turned toward my father. "He's someone I met on the bus to New York. He trying to break into the music industry as a manager."

"Can he? Can he get you in the industry? Is he any good?"

"He's already secured her a good and solid deal."

"Lorraine, honey, maybe you should reconsider this." My father said.

"How do you know it's a good deal?" I asked, looking directly at Kevin.

"The same way I know about the letter. He came to the boutique to see me. I was pretty nasty toward him. But he said something to me that made me see things differently."

"What did he say?"

"He made me realize that it wasn't fair for me to ask you not to follow your dreams, just because I was scared of what it might do to you— to us. I didn't want to admit it, but he was right. I was chasing my dream, why shouldn't you. Why can't we chase our dreams together? He said that if I really loved you, then I wouldn't do something that could cause you to resent me later.

"He told me about the deal he had secured with Misty. I didn't believe him, so I called her and asked to see it."

"So, it is a good deal?" My father asked.

Kevin, looked at me. "To be honest, it's better than the deal Mrs. D got for Semeerah."

"Who's Semeerah, Sister?"

"She's the daughter of Mrs. D, the lady who helped me get to New York.

"She's a singer too?" Ella asked.

"She is. In fact, daddy would buy me her Cd's, whenever a new one came out."

"You're not talking about that Semeerah, are you?"

"I am." I saw the strange look on daddy's face.

"Is her mother's name, Dena Fox?"

"It is. You know Mrs. D?"

"I only saw her once, and it was briefly. Have you and Semeerah met?"

"We have. We met for the first time, yesterday. Why?"

He stood up.

"Daddy, what is it? Why do you have that look on your face? It's the same look you had when you told me that..."

The door opened, and a woman walked in.

"That you were adopted." She said.

I turned toward her. Our eyes locked in on each other. "Who are you?" I whispered.

The question lingered on my lips, and when it finally reached her—she opened her hand.

It was there. The gold locket.

I didn't take my eyes off her as I struggled to open the purse that hung at my side.

When my fingers finally had a good grasp on the key, the tears came.

She took the key from me.

I heard the locket click open.

That's when it stopped. Time.

The walls grew silent. The lights stood still.

Two teardrops hit the floor.

Hers. Mine.

Her body began to move toward me. Time stepped aside.

Our fingers touched as she placed the open locket in my hand.

I was afraid to look down. Afraid to take my eyes off her.

They were hazel.

Hazel eyes, just like mine.

"Breathe." She said.

"How?"

"Slowly, as you look at it."

"I can't."

"You have to."

I finally shifted my eyes from her. My head tilted down, and I stared at the open locket. I saw it.

"My name is Honour Blue Baker, I'm your mother."

The locket slipped from my fingers. I watched it hit the floor. She reached down and picked it up. Her lips began to move again. Her words glided through the air and landed in a spot where, for that moment, only she, me and the locket existed.

Her hand reached out and touched the locket. Resting on the picture inside. "The other baby that I'm holding, she is your twin sister. Her name is Semeerah."

FORTY-NINE
Honour Blue Baker

The sun placed a peck upon my cheek as I glanced up and saw him. He stood with his hands neatly tucked at his side. He looked handsome in the well-tailored black tuxedo that my soon-to-be, son-in-law so carefully crafted.

Our eyes met as I reached the middle of the bridge. The Thompson Mill Bridge.

On this day, my dress was made out of peace.

My veil was decorated with lace and happiness.

My ring was wrapped in the words of eternity and the love of my life, was waiting to marry me.

My two daughters stood together on my left. Their harmonized voices traveling through the air, digging into the roots of trees and causing their branches to stretch out, just to have a listen.

It had taken us time, but we moved forward. A year had passed, but we made it. We made it to this moment.

I held the hand of my grandson as I moved in this moment.

This moment that was filled with hope. That was caressed by love. That had seen justice. Had wiped away tears and brought about smiles.

I welcomed this moment.

Mama's fish swam alongside me as if they were walking me down the aisle as well. I promised myself that I wouldn't cry. But it was hard not to. I missed her.

They say she woke up and demanded a piece of paper and a pen. They say she had written for ten minutes before the pen dropped from her hand and she took her last breath.

I didn't get to say good-bye.

But she did.

FIFTY
Emma Lee Baker

Dear Honour,

I'm about to take my last breath.

I suppose not everybody gets to write down their last thoughts before they die. But since you know I always got to get the last word; I'm writing this down for you baby girl. I reckon that's something. In the end, I figure we all still trying to find something to leave behind, something that reminds folks that we once walked the good ground and took a deep breath for seventy or eighty years. I ain't gonna lie; my last thoughts are probably something one wishes they could keep locked up inside them. Shoot, you probably wondering why I'm telling it. Heck, I reckon right about now, you're wondering why I don't just take it with me. I don't know really. I guess I just felt like I was tired of trying to find the right forgiving water to stop the hurt.

As my daddy used to say, "Truth, let the heart speak it."

I know I quote from him a lot. But that's what good hand-me-down wisdom does for you. I hope I handed some down to you that you can use.

I pray I'm going to give you something to keep in that beautiful heart of yours.

Anywho, I was supposed to be telling you something, so I reckon I better get on with it.

My truth.

I didn't believe you at first. I didn't believe the truth that dripped from the lips of my child. But I need you to know baby girl...I need you to know that in the end, I believed everything and I was sorry.

I was sorry that I didn't see it. That I wasn't looking close enough.

To see what he had done to you.

I wish I could tell him how ugly he is or was. I wish I could stare Into the eyes of the man that tried to take everything away from a young girl who had everything to live for.

But he didn't take everything.

Your daddy and I gave you something that he could never take. That's courage and love.

Courage ain't something to sneeze at. It's a precious gift that many would pay for. They would pay to have it in their bones. But courage can't be brought.

Courage is what holds your bones together. It's their strength.

It can only be shown.

Live on that Honour, love will come and see you through the rest.

Don't turn love away. Don't run away from it. Don't allow it to keep running down the street looking for a home. Love, Honour, needs a home. A home that can be broken into.

None of us welcomes thieves. But you want your heart to be stolen, Honour. Give it to the man that will never return it.

The man that will always see its worth.

Kiss Bryan for me on your wedding day.

Feed my fish.

Find your freedom from the past.

It ain't gonna be easy to not look back at it. But only look back to the parts that made your future look like red roses.

I always say that red roses are worth stopping and taking a moment to show appreciation for their beauty.

Tell Jimmy that I done forgave him.

This last part that I'm writing be for my granddaughters.

Semeerah and Lorraine. You tell them that I love them. I ain't never laid my eyes on them, but I know they be beautiful, 'cause they done come from you Honour.

My daddy used to say, "tomorrow, you may not be where you want to be, but at least your feet are moving; so that you ain't standing in the same spot you were yesterday."

It will take them time. Keep your feet moving, Honour. Drag them girls along with ya, if you have too.

Daughters always forget that they mama's ain't perfect. A mama's love is perfect, but their actions, ain't always so.

Tell them, that I speak from experience.

I love you baby girl.

Mama

P.S. You tell Nurse Rosa that she had better be glad she put my locket back.

READER'S GUIDE - DISCUSSION QUESTIONS

1. At the beginning of the novel, we see a letter written by Emma Lee Baker to her daughter. If you could write your own 'good-bye' letter, what would you include? Would you disclose secrets? What would you want people to remember about you?

2. Emma discussing the close bond between her daughter, Honour, and the father, Jean. Do you feel that the close bond between fathers and daughters still exist today? If so, why? If not, how do you think this can be changed?

3. Do you think some people get to the point that they forget their roots? If so, why do you think this occurs?

4. Emma describes her relationship with Honour as "burnt toast and year-old jam," do you think this was accurate?

5. Describe what 'freedom' looks like to you?

6. Can a person ever get over sexual assault? Do you feel that after twenty-three years, Honour should have been able to move forward?

7. What do you think Honour's biggest fear was?

8. Do you think Honour should have forgiven Aaron?

9. Which one did you choose for Honour? Aaron or Bryan? Talk about why.

10. Who proposed better, Aaron or Bryan?

11. Do you believe in love at first sight? If not, why not? If so, have you experienced it?

12. Did you feel that Kevin was abusive? What was your impression of him at the end?

13. What were your thoughts on Ms. M? Do you think she will ever trust a man? Did you feel she was wrong about Kevin?

14. What did you think about Lorraine's father? About Ole Big Bones?

15. Was Lorraine too trusting? What were her strengths? What were her weaknesses?

16. What were your thoughts on David? Did you feel Lorraine should have given him a second chance?

17. Did you feel that Kevin's thoughts about the music industry were correct? Did you think he was still in love with Sameerah?

18. Mrs. D believed in helping people 'move forward.' Do you feel that people have gotten away from helping each other? What did you like about Mrs. D? Did she remind you of anyone in your life that helped you? If you had a Mrs. D in your life, do you feel obligated to help others?

19. What did you know about the 'one-drop' rule? Do you feel it still exists today?

20. Do you feel that Honour finally found her peace?

www.ingramcontent.com/pod-product-compliance
Lightning Source LLC
Chambersburg PA
CBHW030520310726
48979CB00010B/1737/J

* 9 7 8 0 6 1 5 4 4 1 5 5 9 *